The
Blossoms Meet
the
Vulture
Lady

The Blossoms Meet the Vulture Lady

BETSY BYARS

Illustrated by Jacqueline Rogers

Delacorte
Press

Published by
Delacorte Press
Bantam Doubleday Dell Publishing Group, Inc.
666 Fifth Avenue
New York, N.Y. 10103

Text copyright © 1986 by Betsy Byars

Illustrations copyright © 1986 by Jacqueline Rogers

The Trademark Delacorte Press® is registered in the U.S.
Patent and Trademark Office.
Manufactured in the United States of America

9   8   7   6

Library of Congress Cataloging in Publication Data
Byars, Betsy Cromer.
  The Blossoms meet the vulture lady.

  Summary: When Junior accidentally gets caught in his
own coyote trap deep in the woods, he is rescued by the
reclusive woman known as Mad Mary and begins an
unforgettable adventure.
  [1. Friendship—Fiction]   2. Prejudices—Fiction.
3. Family life—Fiction]   I. Rogers, Jackie, ill.
II. Title.
PZ7.B9836B1   1986   [Fic]
ISBN 0-385-29485-9
Library of Congress Catalog Card Number: 86-4429

The
Blossoms Meet
the
Vulture
Lady

Chapter One

The Thing Under the Tarp

❧ ❧ ❧

"I'M FINISHED!" JUNIOR CALLED.

He walked to the barn door and looked out. No one was in sight.

"I'm finished! Hey, you can see it now! Where are you guys?"

No answer.

Junior walked out into the sunlight. He made a visor of one hand.

Nobody was in the yard.

"I said I'm finished," he yelled at the top of his lungs. "You can see it now!"

Still no answer.

Junior sighed. All morning long he had been wasting valuable construction time keeping Maggie and Vern out of the barn, keeping them from seeing what he was working on. Every time he turned his back, one of them would try to sneak in the door. "Oh, no you don't." Or slip through the loose board in the back of the barn.

He must have said "Oh, no you don't" at least a hundred times.

1

All the yelling had made his mom come out of the house. "What's Junior doing in the barn?" he heard her say.

"I don't know. He won't let us see," Maggie said. "He's making something."

"And he's using all of Pap's hog wire," Vern said.

"Junior, are you making anything dangerous in there?"

"No'm."

"What is it?"

"It's a surprise."

"Well, I've had enough of your surprises. Come out here. We have just gotten through paying for your last summer's surprise—flying off the barn. Come out here this minute."

Junior appeared in the doorway of the barn. He had a hammer in one hand.

"I didn't fly," he explained, "I fell."

"What are you making in there now?" Vicki Blossom's hands went on her hips.

Junior sighed. He walked reluctantly to his mother and said, "I'm making a . . ." Then he lowered his voice and whispered the rest of it.

"A what?"

He sent a suspicious glance in Maggie and Vern's direction to make sure they couldn't hear. He cupped his hands around his mother's ear. "A . . ." he said.

"But why? What for? Hurry up, Junior. I've got a customer inside. I'm cornrowing her hair and customers don't grow on trees."

Junior sighed again. "Remember last night? Remember . . ." He motioned for her to bend down again. This time he gave such a long explanation that Maggie and Vern started slipping to the back of the barn where the loose board was.

"Oh, no you don't."

He had run into the barn and thrown a tarp over his invention. "There! Spy all you want to." From then on he'd worked strictly under the tarp. It had been hot under there and the air smelled of old oil, but Junior felt it was worth it.

Now, after all that, he was finished, and there was no one around to see what he had made.

Junior glanced down at his watch even though the watch was broken. According to this watch, the time was always 3:05. When Junior had first found the watch in the parking lot of Sears and strapped it on his arm, he'd kept hoping that one time he would glance down and it would say 3:06, but he had given up on that now. Still, he looked at his watch every time he was curious about the time, like right now. Maybe Maggie and Vern were eating lunch or something.

"Why do you wear that old broken watch?" Maggie had once asked. "It never gives you the right time."

"It does too," he had answered. "At three-oh-five in the afternoon and three-oh-five at night."

Anyway, he liked the way he looked with a watch on his wrist.

He checked the time again. With a sigh, he walked back to the barn. He stood in the doorway, looking at the bulging tarp.

Well, if Maggie and Vern weren't interested enough

to wait, they just weren't going to get to see it. He would set it up without them. It would serve them right.

He felt better after he had made that decision. He got the wheelbarrow from the corner and rolled it over to the tarp. He lifted the tarp dramatically, the way he had intended lifting it for Maggie and Vern.

He said, "Ta-daaaa!"

He gasped with pleasure. Just in the few minutes it had been out of his sight, it had gotten more impressive. He was smitten with regret that Maggie and Vern weren't there to admire it.

His invention was spectacular—as sturdy as if it had been made by a real carpenter. He walked around it. From every side it was a beautiful, professional job. The word *professional* said it all.

The hog wire was fitted over the top, nailed neatly into place; the nail heads hammered sideways over the wire for extra security. The corner boards had been put into place with screws—more security. Even he himself —the inventor—would not be able to get out if he was locked inside. That's how professional it was.

"And," he said, speaking aloud to his invention, "you're going to make me rich."

He loaded his creation awkwardly onto the wheelbarrow. It tipped and he straightened it with his knee. Hog wire took off some skin.

Now he really wished Maggie and Vern were there— this time to take a corner. Even without them the invention finally thudded solidly onto the wheelbarrow.

Junior secured it with rope, making a bow on top as if it were a present.

He glanced out the barn door to make sure Maggie and Vern had not returned without his hearing them. That would be just like them—to spy on his invention and then run away without praising it. No, the yard was empty.

"Where are they?"

For a moment he considered pushing it just to the edge of the woods and waiting until they returned. That would give them a chance to see him, just a glimpse of him and his beautiful, professional creation, and then he would disappear into the woods.

He thought longingly of their envious cries: "Junior, what is that?" "Junior, where did you get that?" And the final, disbelieving "Is that what you were making? Come back, Junior. Please let us see."

He lingered over the thought. He wanted to hear those words a lot, but he didn't have time. There was still work to do. He glanced at his watch: 3:05. He would have to hurry to be finished by supper.

Quickly he pushed the wheelbarrow out of the barn. Legs flashing in the sunlight, he headed for the house. He ran in, and in a few minutes he ran out. There was a bulge in his back pocket.

Then Junior picked up the wheelbarrow handles and ran hard for the woods.

Chapter Two

Mad Mad Mary

❦   ❦   ❦

"Go 'way! Shoo!"

Mad Mary stepped onto the highway. "Shoo!" She waved her arms. Her torn sleeves flapped in the still air.

The two vultures looked her way. They had the carcass of a rabbit between them. They had opened it quickly by pulling in opposite directions. One vulture dropped its part, the head, spread its wings as if to take to the air, and then changed its mind and folded them.

Mad Mary was still a hundred yards down the road, no real threat as yet. They knew Mad Mary and were used to competing with her for highway meat.

The vulture lowered its bald head to the rabbit.

But Mad Mary was running over the shimmering asphalt now, closing the distance. "I said 'Shoo!' " She threatened them with her cane.

One vulture hissed. The other took a few steps across the road, but leisurely, like a barnyard turkey. The hissing vulture dug its beak quickly into the meat and picked at the dead rabbit. It got hold of a piece of intestine and pulled.

"I want that rabbit!"

Mad Mary flew at them. Now she was close enough to be a threat. Four more strides and she would be able to hook one of the vultures around the neck with the end of her long cane. Both vultures ran down the road, building up speed, and took to the air.

Mad Mary ran a few feet beyond the dead rabbit. She watched the vultures settle on the limb of a nearby tree. Then she eased the rabbit over with the toe of her boot.

"Fresh meat," she muttered to herself.

Then she lifted her head. She heard the sound of an approaching truck.

Leaning down, she picked up the rabbit with one hand. The vultures had popped it open and pulled out part of the insides. Other than that, the rabbit was perfect. Mad Mary liked to get meat that hadn't been run over five or six times. It was juicier.

Like the fat possum she had found last week and dined off for two days, the rabbit had just taken a light bump on the head from some rear tire. The body was still limber—couldn't have been dead twenty minutes. She slid the rabbit down into her stained shoulder bag.

The truck was blaring its horn. The driver had spotted Mad Mary.

Mad Mary didn't even glance in the truck's direction. She walked leisurely to the edge of the road and stepped off into the grass. Then, head down, poking the ground with her long shepherd's cane, she moved along with steady soldier strides.

The truck blew its horn again as it passed. Mad Mary

felt the exhaust, the sting of dust, but she did not look up. There was nobody in the whole world that she wanted to see. She hadn't even nodded to a living soul in three and a half years.

The vultures watched from separate limbs of a nearby dead tree. When the truck passed, they flew down to the spot where the rabbit had lain. They checked to see if Mad Mary had left them anything. Then, although she had not, they continued to walk around the damp spot on the highway for a few moments.

As they took to the air again, Mad Mary turned the curve of the highway, jumped the ditch, and headed into the woods.

Chapter Three

The Hamburger Ball

❧   ❧   ❧

"I just figured out what it is," Maggie said.

She and Vern were at the creek. Maggie was sitting on the raised bank swinging her legs out over the water. Vern was making little rafts out of twigs and vines and sending them down the shallow, shifting current, watching them plunge over the waterfall.

"What what is?"

He released his fourth raft and frowned as it headed for the willow tree.

"I bet I know what Junior's making."

"What?"

His raft was caught against the roots of the tree. He could barely see it through the curtain of willow branches. He waded across, parted the branches, and got his raft.

Vern enjoyed making small things. He spent money every Saturday for a plastic model, but no matter how hard a model he got, he was always finished by Sunday.

"Well, if you're not interested, I'm not going to waste

my breath telling you," Maggie said, turning away. She stuck a blade of grass in her mouth.

"I'm interested. What's he making?"

"Oh, all right. He's making a trap."

"A trap?" Vern looked at her for the first time. "What kind of trap?"

"Coyote."

"Come on. Even Junior's got better sense than to set a trap for a coyote. That's like setting a trap for a polar bear or . . ." He paused to repair a loose vine. "Or a crocodile."

"Weren't you listening last night at supper? Yesterday Pap heard on the news about a coyote that's loose in the area. They think it got away from Farmer Brown's Zoo, only Farmer Brown won't admit it because it's been killing people's chickens and lambs, and he doesn't want to have to pay." She slung her braids behind her shoulders with one practiced shake of her head. "Junior wants the reward."

"How much is it?"

"A hundred dollars."

"Shoot, for a hundred dollars I'd make a trap myself."

Vern's last raft had now gone successfully over the fall, and Vern watched his fleet of rafts, four of them, sailing down the creek, moving in and out of the long shadows of the trees.

"Are you really going to make a trap?" Maggie asked. "I'll help."

"No, I'm helping Pap this afternoon."

"Doing what?"

"Collecting cans."

11

Every Monday afternoon Pap went around the county collecting beer and pop cans that people had thrown out of car windows and left at picnic sites. It was his job, the most satisfying he had ever had. He started when he wanted, quit when he wanted, and got paid for what he collected. Vern was his assistant.

"Oh, I forgot it was Monday. Anyway, Junior probably used up all the hog wire. Did you see how big his trap was? Big enough for a pony."

"Junior never was one to conserve."

"No."

Vern's rafts were out of sight now, on their way—he liked to think—to the ocean. He imagined them bobbing in the first gentle ripples of the tide, then riding the curling waves out to sea. Although he had never actually seen the ocean, the picture was clearer than a lot of things he had seen.

He climbed out of the creek without using his hands, by digging his toes into the cool slimy mud and turning his feet sideways to take advantage of rock and root ledges. At the top he waved his arms in the air in a rare moment of imbalance.

Seeing her advantage, Maggie yelled, "Race you!" She broke into a run for the barn.

"That's not fair. I wasn't ready!" he called after her. Then he couldn't help himself. He broke into a run and began to overtake her.

Mud was following Junior into the woods. Three times Junior had turned around, hands on hips, and said "Go home, Mud. Go home! I mean it. Go home!"

So Mud knew he was not wanted. Still he followed. He could not help himself. He knew Junior had a ball of raw hamburger meat in his back pocket.

Mud had been lying under the kitchen table, taking a nap, when Junior slipped into the house. Without opening his eyes, Mud knew it was Junior. Junior in the hall . . . Junior in the dining room . . . Junior in the kitchen. When it was Junior opening the refrigerator door, Mud opened his eyes.

Junior was on a straight chair, reaching into the freezer. Mud crawled out from under the table, stretched, and sat attentively.

Junior took out a frozen package of something and began working on it with a butcher knife. Finally Junior cut off a chunk. Frozen chips sprayed onto the linoleum floor.

Mud moseyed over. He smelled one, licked it up. Hamburger! It was hamburger! Mud's nose began to run.

Raw hamburger was Mud's favorite thing to eat in the world. The only time he got it was when Pap wrapped it around a worm pill. "Catch!" Pap would say. Mud always caught. He thought all balls of hamburger came with a hard, foul-tasting center that you weren't allowed to spit out, but still he loved it.

With eager care Mud sniffed the floor until he was sure he had gotten every crumb. By then Junior was gone.

Mud pushed open the screen door with his front paws, bounded out, and, ears flapping, ran for the woods. He could not see Junior, but the faint scent of hamburger followed Junior like a wake.

He caught up with Junior in the pine trees. "Go home!" Junior said immediately.

Mud was surprised. He was almost never sent back to the house. He sat down.

"I did not say 'Sit,' I said 'Go home!' "

Mud pretended to obey. He took a few steps toward the house. When Junior was once again pushing his wheelbarrow, Mud followed again.

Junior spun around. "I said 'Go home!' Watch my lips. Go home! I do not want you scaring off my coyote. Go home."

Again, Mud pretended to obey. Then, again, he followed. Sooner or later Junior would break down and give him a piece of hamburger meat.

Following as closely as he dared, nose wet with desire, Mud went deeper into the woods.

Chapter Four

Following Junior

❧ ❧ ❧

MAGGIE CAME UP SHORT AT THE DOOR OF THE BARN.
"Where did Junior go?" she asked.

Hopping on one foot, she picked a burr from the side
of the other. Vern ran past her and tagged the sagging
barn door. "I won!"

"You did not. I quit!"

"Well, I didn't."

"That's your problem." Maggie spit on her finger and
cleaned the spot where the burr had been. She looked
closely at the round clean spot on her dusty foot. Then
she glanced up at Vern. "So where do you think Junior
went?"

"He probably went to set his trap." Vern walked forward, looking carefully at the ground. "See, here are
wheelbarrow tracks."

They followed the dusty trail with their eyes. "He
went to the house, probably to get something—bait,
most likely—and then he headed for the woods." Vern
always seemed to have a sixth sense about Junior.

They put their hands over their eyes so they could see the trail as it curled beyond the old rosebushes. "Let's follow it and see where he went. Want to?" Maggie asked. "Maybe we can find some kind of joke animal to put in the trap—that would be funny—a turtle or something. A skunk would be perfect, but I know we can't—"

Pap came out of the house yawning. He paused on the top step to stretch. "Vern, you ready to go?" he called across the yard.

"I been ready."

"Maggie, you want to come?"

Maggie hesitated. It would be more fun to follow Junior's trail into the woods, but only if Vern or somebody was along for company. This summer, being alone didn't give her as much pleasure as it used to.

"Oh, all right." She moved closer to the pickup truck. Then she yelled, "But I get to sit by the window," and she broke into a run.

"I sit by the window!"

"First one there gets it!"

Maggie ran across the yard and jumped on the running board. Vern was struggling with Pap's door while Maggie struggled with hers. They got them open at the same minute, but Maggie ended up in the window seat and Vern behind the steering wheel. Maggie grinned.

Pap came to the car, looking from left to right. "Where's Mud?" he asked. "Anybody seen Mud?"

"He probably followed Junior," Vern said. Reluctantly he slid over so Pap could get in. He hated to ride in the middle. It was unmanly.

"Followed Junior? Where?"

"Into the woods."

Pap paused. Every day, when he took his after-lunch nap, Mud took a nap, too, under the kitchen table. It was an unusual thing for Mud not to be waiting right there when Pap got up.

Pap climbed into the truck and swept the empty yard with one final glance. "This ain't like Mud. He knows it's can-collecting day."

Pap sounded Mud's signal on the horn of the pickup: one long, two shorts. He waited. He sounded it again.

"Well, if he don't want to go . . ." Pap sounded hurt. He started the engine and steered the pickup out of the yard. On the timber bridge he paused to sound the horn one last time. Then the truck bounced over the rutted road toward the highway and disappeared into the pines.

"I said 'Go home!' "

Junior turned again and put his hands on his hips, his mom's pose when she meant business. He glared at Mud. Mud slunk toward the nearest tree. Head and tail lowered, he watched Junior through the leaves.

Junior nodded his head for emphasis. "And I mean it. No coyote in his right mind wants to be around dogs."

Junior turned. Actually he loved for people to follow him, even to spy on him. It was flattering. He heard Mud's footsteps behind him, and he grimaced with false annoyance. He loved to have to tell people again and again to leave him alone. His saddest moments were when they did.

"I mean it, Mud," he sang out, this time without turning. He pushed the wheelbarrow over some tree roots and cried "Whoa" when it almost tipped. When it didn't fall, he said to the invention, "Don't scare me like that."

Mud was coming slower now. He was ashamed. He had been told to go home so many times that it had made him feel bad, genuinely unwelcome.

Suddenly far away, in the distance, he heard the truck horn. It was his beep—one long, two shorts. His ears snapped up. His head lifted.

Junior swirled. He heard the horn, too, and he knew he was in danger of losing his only audience. He swirled and reached for his back pocket as quickly as a gunfighter in a showdown.

"I got something for you," he said. He knelt.

Mud's head was up; he was listening. He heard the sound of the horn again. Wrinkles appeared in his forehead.

Junior rattled the paper as he opened the ball of hamburger. "See, it's hamburger. You want some hamburger? Your favorite, Mud, ground round."

Mud hesitated. He wagged his tail, but it was at half mast. Junior pinched off a piece and held it out so Mud could smell it. "Here you go."

Mud came forward. His nose was running. He couldn't help himself. He accepted the small pinch of hamburger meat and swallowed it. His golden eyes watched the rest of the meat in Junior's hand.

Junior twisted his fingers around Mud's bandanna so Mud couldn't pull away if he wanted to. He put the

18

meat in his pocket and patted it. "There's more where that came from," he said. When he realized he had Mud's full attention, he released his bandanna and stood up. He picked up the wheelbarrow handles and pushed.

The horn sounded again—one long, two shorts. Junior put his hand in his back pocket and rattled the hamburger paper.

Once again, Mud couldn't help himself. He followed.

Chapter Five

Mad Mary

🌿   🌿   🌿

SINCE MAGGIE WAS BY THE WINDOW, SHE WAS THE first to spot Mad Mary. "There she is! There she is!"

"Who?" Vern asked without interest. He was still unhappy about having to sit in the middle. Usually his only competition for the window seat was Mud, and they shared.

"Mad Mary!"

Vern leaned forward. His mouth dropped open. Maggie had said the one word that could cause him to look out the window. He had promised himself he would not look out HER window no matter what or whom she saw. But he could not miss a chance to see Mad Mary. He leaned across his sister.

Mad Mary was standing at the side of the road. She was looking at something in her hand, something she had just taken up from the road. She stuffed it in the bag she kept slung over her shoulder, and without a glance at the pickup truck, she started walking.

Mad Mary was known for her cane—a long stick,

20

curved at the top like a shepherd's hook. Kids were scared of that hook. "She'll grab you with it if you get close," they said, and they believed it. The cane moved like part of Mad Mary, an extra arm or leg. She was never seen without it.

"What was that she put in her bag?" Vern asked. He spoke in a whisper even though she was too far away to hear him. He had always had a dread of Mad Mary. If he was by himself when he saw her, he ran into the woods rather than pass her.

"I couldn't see. It was either a dead squirrel or a rabbit. It was too flat to tell."

"She'll eat it," Vern said. "She doesn't care what it is. She'll eat skunk."

"Maybe she doesn't eat it," Maggie said, leaning back thoughtfully. "Maybe she just collects it to make potions and stuff, magic spells."

"She eats it," Pap said.

Maggie leaned around Vern to look at him. "Pap, people in my school says she's a witch."

"She's no witch. I went to school with her."

"You went to school with Mad Mary?"

Both Maggie and Vern were leaning forward now, staring at Pap. Both mouths were open.

Pap nodded. He steered the pickup into a picnic area and pulled on the brakes.

"What was she like, Pap?"

"Back then I don't remember her being no different from anybody else," Pap said. "Except that her family had more money than anybody in the county and they always kept to themselves. Now let's pick up cans if we're going to pick up cans."

"How do you know she eats the stuff, Pap?" Maggie said, sliding out. The seats of the pickup were worn as slick as a sliding board.

"We had a conversation one time. I was getting pop bottles—it was bottles back then. You got two cents apiece for them. I was walking along looking for bottles and I came on Mary. She was scraping up something off the road. DORs she calls them, dead-on-roads."

"Gross," Maggie said.

"She thinks of it as dried meat—sun-dried meat. She said it's better than beef jerky. 'Course, most of the time she cooks her meat—varmint stew, she makes."

"Supergross," Maggie said.

"She invited me over one time."

"To her house?"

Pap nodded. "She was more sociable in those days. 'I make the best varmint stew in the county,' she said. I said, 'It would have to go some to beat my mama's varmint stew. It was known statewide. You put red peppers in yours?' 'Red and green if I got them,' she said. We went on like that for a while, swapping recipes, and then she went her way and I went mine."

Maggie and Vern were staring at him as if he didn't have good sense. Finally Maggie shook her head in disbelief. "Pap, let me get this straight. Mad Mary invited you over to her house?"

"Yep." Pap opened a bag of trash in the first container and pulled out two Diet Pepsi cans.

"Where does she live?"

"At that time she lived in an old shack by the river. She built it herself, built it out of what was left of the old home place after it burned. Then she had to move when they put in the dam. After that she got less sociable, talked to herself instead of other people. I don't know where she lives now—in the woods somewhere."

"Did you go to the old shack, Pap?"

"No, I never got around to it."

Maggie shook her head in amazement. "I wish you'd gone. Then you could tell us about it."

"Well, I didn't, so I can't."

"Anyway, people in my school say she's a witch."

"I've heard that too," Vern said.

Pap was going through the second trash can. "Plastic bottles," he said, his voice deep with disgust. "I hate them things." He moved on. "Ah," he said at the next can. "Here we go."

He began dropping can after can into his plastic bag. He smiled. The sound of pop cans falling into a plastic sack was music to his ears.

"Here she comes! Here she comes!" Maggie said.

This time Vern didn't have to ask who. He turned and watched as Mad Mary, hook in hand, made her way toward the picnic area. Unconsciously he stepped closer to Pap.

"She's coming, Pap," Maggie said. She tugged his sleeve. "Say hey to her. See if she remembers you."

Pap paused to open a Kentucky Fried Chicken box and shake out two cans. "I wish people wouldn't hide their cans," Pap said. He wiped chicken grease on the bib of his overalls. "It's messy to have to—"

"Pap!" Maggie said urgently. Pap glanced up.

Mad Mary was passing the picnic area. She was looking straight ahead, her sharp profile angled against the woods beyond. Her wide-brimmed straw hat hid most of her face and all of her gray hair.

"Afternoon, Mary," Pap said. He touched his hand to his forehead where the brim of his hat would have been if he had had one on.

Mad Mary did not answer. She did not change her stride or the rhythm of her cane. She just kept walking.

Pap shook his head. "Ever since they took her shack away from her, she sure ain't been sociable."

Pap threw the bag into the back of the pickup. "Let's go."

Chapter Six
The Six-Second Nightmare

🌿 🌿 🌿

THE COYOTE TRAP WAS HIDDEN DEEP IN THE BLACK-berry bushes, perfectly camouflaged. It was exactly the sort of spot, Junior thought, that a coyote would be looking for.

He stood for a moment, wiping his dusty hands on his T-shirt, admiring the way the trap blended into the leaves. Not even a coyote would spot the wire, the trapdoor.

It would seem like an ordinary little cave in the leaves, Junior thought, a bower. The coyote would hurry in, circle a few times, and then collapse the way Mud collapsed under the kitchen table. It was so perfect that Junior felt he did not even have to put the bait inside for an enticement.

Junior's beautiful dream continued.

The coyote would lie there, panting at first, licking his dusty paws, enjoying the retreat. Then he would smell the hamburger meat. All animals loved hamburger, so Junior knew he was safe using that. He would smell the hamburger, lift his head, spot the beautiful ball of meat, crouch down, smell it, take it gingerly into his mouth, and at that moment the spring would snap, the door would fall, the latch would click.

Hello, Coyote.

It made Junior's blood race to think of it.

He reached into his pocket where he had the hamburger meat still wrapped in the freezer paper. Carefully he unwrapped it. It smelled good. Junior inhaled the odor. Fresh. It was still frozen a little in the center, but Junior was sure that by the time the coyote came, it would be soft all the way through.

In his mind the coyote he would catch was the one he watched on Saturday-morning cartoons, the one with lots of expressions. Junior knew exactly which expression the coyote would be wearing when Junior arrived tomorrow, that sort of sheepish, well-you-got-me smile he wore when things didn't go right. Maybe he would even give one of those comical shrugs.

And when Junior opened the door, the coyote, resigned to capture, would walk out on his hind legs, like a person. Junior grinned.

He got down on his hands and knees. Over his head was the trapdoor, strung up by fishing line. Junior had chosen fishing line because it was almost invisible. Even he who knew it was there could hardly spot it.

The trapdoor was straight up and balanced so finely that it took almost nothing to trigger it; just a touch of the hamburger triggering device would be enough. Junior was proud of that. He was going to put the hamburger meat between tin-can lids, like a tin-can-lid sandwich. And inside the hamburger meat would be the string. If the coyote even sniffed hard at the tin-can sandwich, it could go off, and if he touched it . . .

With great care he crawled into the trap. He had spent a lot of time pushing dirt into the trap, covering the edges of wood, and he didn't want to disturb it.

Inside, he turned and paused for a minute to imagine it once again from the coyote's viewpoint. It was irresistible. The coyote would be overjoyed to find this wonderful place. It was roomy enough for a half dozen coyotes, one of the nicest traps Junior had ever seen in his life. He hoped that after he made the capture, the reporters would get a picture of him standing beside the trap. He shuddered with sudden, intense pleasure.

There was a little dirt on the hamburger meat—Junior had been careless while he was crawling in—and he brushed it off. Only the best for his coyote.

Junior crossed his legs—there wasn't room for him to sit erect, so he bent over, facing the back of the trap. This was the most important moment—the setting of the trap. The door overhead was very sensitive, ready to snap shut and lock at the slightest movement.

He drew in his breath. His tongue flicked over his dry lips.

He began to roll the hamburger in his hands, as if it were clay. He paused for a moment to admire it. It was as round and smooth as a tennis ball.

In the shadows of the pine trees Mud watched. His nose began to run. He moved closer to the trap. Junior was too intent to notice. He took the string. He took it very, very carefully because the trapdoor was so sensitive, he didn't want to . . . Again he held his breath. He pressed the string into the soft meat.

Now he pulled out the tin-can lids. One was tuna, one was tomato soup. Junior had not rinsed either one because—who knows?—tuna and tomato soup might be just what the coyote ordered. Junior smiled.

Then slowly, very, very carefully, Junior squeezed the hamburger meat between the two lids. Perfect. It couldn't be better. He set the tin-can sandwich at the back of the cage. Perfect. Now all he had to do was back very, very slowly out of the trap.

He swallowed. His excitement was so great, he was almost choking on it.

He started backing out. It almost seemed that the trapdoor trembled above him. "Not yet," he told the door. "Wait for the—"

He never got to utter the word *coyote*. He felt hot breath on his bare leg. He screamed. The coyote had filled his mind so completely for the past hour, he had no doubts that the coyote was here.

He lunged back into the trap. He spun around. It was Mud. Mud was just as startled as Junior and had run halfway across the clearing with his tail between his legs.

Junior glanced up at the trapdoor. It was still there, straight up. "Thank you, thank you," he told it. Then the intense relief he was feeling died. He discovered that his hand was on the tin-can sandwich. He had squashed it flat.

Again he muttered a "Thank you" to the trapdoor. He lifted his hand. He was horrified to see the tin-can sandwich come up with it. The next three seconds were a nightmare.

The trapdoor swished down through the leaves like the blade of a guillotine. Leaves, blackberries, bugs, flew through the hot summer air. Then there was the terrible final double click as the trapdoor locked into place.

Hello, Junior.

Chapter Seven

Blackberry Time

❧   ❧   ❧

MAD MARY WADED THROUGH THE CREEK WITHOUT
bothering to keep her boots dry. The creek ran cold
even in July, but Mad Mary did not notice the icy water
leaking in through the worn soles, soaking her socks.

When Mad Mary was a girl, the family had had a
servant to polish their shoes and wash and iron their
shoelaces. Now her laces were so knotted and caked
with mud, she never untied them. If she ever had to
take off her boots, she would cut them out and start
over.

She stepped up the creek bank in one long practiced
stride. Her stick dug into the mud for support. The old
cloth bag bobbed against her shoulder.

Mad Mary cut through the bushes using her cane to
push back the leaves, first on one side, then on the
other. The cloth of her skirts was so worn that even the
sharpest thorns could not get a tight enough hold to
delay her.

At the edge of the clearing she paused. Her bright
eyes raked the ground.

31

She closed her right eye. That was her weak eye, and she always closed it when she wanted to see something more clearly.

The look in her left eye sharpened. Her nostrils flared. There they were. Onions. Wild onions. She was there in four steps.

"A rabbit, a squirrel, and onions," she muttered to herself. "I'll eat good tonight." She always felt that her stews were better, richer, if there were at least two different kinds of meat and lots of onions.

She bent and pulled the onions carefully from the soft ground. She brushed the roots over her skirt to remove the dirt.

When she had gathered a fistful, she turned and poked them into the cloth bag, on top of the two dead animals. The bag had been stained with so many foods, both animal and vegetable, that it had the look of a bag purposefully dyed for camouflage.

Varmint stew, she thought again. It was one of her favorite dishes. Her mouth watered.

Mad Mary had not smiled in ten years. She hadn't seen anything to smile at. The big difference between animals and people, she had once read, is that people can laugh. Well, then, that meant she was more like an animal. It wasn't likely she would ever smile again, much less laugh.

Still, the lines around her eyes eased slightly at the thought of her supper.

There was a roll of thunder, and Mad Mary glanced up at the sky. The clouds overhead were thunder-gray. In the west flashes of lightning lit up the clouds.

Mad Mary watched and then shrugged the bag higher on her shoulder. She was an expert on local weather. She lived with it day and night.

The smell of wild onions was in the air. It overpowered the smell of rain.

She glanced again at the sky. She took another deep breath of onion air. Onions fresh from the ground were the best perfume a person could want.

Then she made her decision. To herself she muttered, "I reckon I got just enough time to gather some blackberries."

Wielding her cane, she headed in that direction.

Chapter Eight
Prob-lem

᪶   ᪶   ᪶

"AND NOBODY'S SEEN JUNIOR?" VICKI BLOSSOM SAID for the third time. Her eyes swept around the table.

Maggie answered. "I told you, Mom. The last time I saw him he was in the barn, under the tarp."

"Me too," said Vern.

"I ain't seen him since breakfast," Pap said.

The Blossom family was at supper. They had been answering this same question since the meal started, but like a detective hoping for a new clue, Vicki Blossom kept asking it.

Now there came a long silence. Vicki Blossom looked out the window. Her hand was pressed against her mouth as if she were trying to hold back a cough.

Under the table Mud chewed a flea on his leg. Mud made a lot of noise when he went after a flea. Then he watched the wet spot of fur for a moment to see if the flea had survived. When he didn't feel anything move beneath the fur, he licked the fur back into place. Then he dropped his head onto his paws.

Maggie dished up a spoonful of popcorn. Monday nights the Blossoms always ate popcorn with milk on it. As she chewed she said, "Vern and I think he went in the woods," she paused to swallow, "to set his trap."

"I thought about that," their mom said. "But that was hours and hours ago."

"So it was a coyote trap, that thing Junior was making?" Vern asked.

"Yes." Vicki Blossom sighed. "He heard Pap say something last night about a reward for a coyote, and he saw himself collecting it." Every time she finished speaking she put her hand against her mouth.

"They thought they caught the coyote," Pap said, "did I tell you?" He paused with a spoonful of popcorn in front of his mouth, the milk dripping back into his bowl. "A motorist claimed he hit it on Route ninety-one. He went to the police station to collect his hundred dollars. He went in carrying the coyote in his arms."

Pap grinned. "Turned out it was a collie he'd hit. Mr. Frank R. Roswell's prize collie. This man hadn't even noticed that his so-called coyote was wearing a collar and dog tags." He wagged his head. "Now he's got to pay for the collie, and prize collies ain't cheap." He shoveled the spoonful of popcorn into his mouth.

Vicki Blossom was still looking out the window.

"Junior will be all night setting that trap, making sure every leaf is just right, every piece of wire in place. Mom, you know how he is," Maggie said. "Junior's a . . ." She paused to spring a new word on the Blossoms. "Perfectionist."

"I know he is, but it's not like him to miss Monday-night supper no matter what he's doing. Popcorn and milk's his favorite."

Nobody could deny that.

There was a sudden roll of thunder, and they all lowered their spoons and looked toward the window. The sun was behind the clouds, and the afternoon had turned dark.

"Storm's coming," Pap said.

"Anyway, I'm not hungry," Maggie said. She threw down her spoon. It clattered on the table.

And as if this were the signal they had been waiting for, the others threw down their spoons, too, and got up from the table.

Junior had only been in the coyote trap six minutes, but the six minutes had been so long and confusing and terrible, he couldn't think straight.

When the trapdoor had first clicked behind him, his mouth had fallen open as if it were connected to the same device. He stared at the door in disbelief. Then he sat back hard and rested his back against the hog-wire side.

"No problem," he told his sinking heart. He closed his eyes and took a deep breath. "No prob-lem."

He pushed against the hog wire with his back. It was just as tight, just as secure as when he had crawled in during its construction and said gleefully, "Nobody could get out of this—not even me, the inventor!"

Well, maybe the hog wire was secure. It had to be to hold hogs. Hogs were strong.

He didn't even want to think of how many nails he had used to secure the superstrong wire—all he had, that's how many, every single nail he could get his hands on. And he had pulled the wire high on the top.

He slid his fingers through the wire mesh and felt the top. He had pulled the wire so tight that he could not even reach the nails. He tried to inch his stubby fingers forward. The wire cut the soft flesh between his fingers, and still he couldn't feel the end.

He pulled his hand in and poked it out at the corner. He could feel the screws at the top, the huge screws that held the four corner supports. He could reach those, but that did him no good. His heart sank lower. The screwdriver was back in the barn.

There was only one answer. He would have to go out the way he had come in: through the door. He licked his dry lips and bent low to inspect the latches.

The door was latched on either side—double latches, and both of them had caught. It hurt him to remember how happy he had been at finding two latches in Pap's junk box. "Double security," he had cried in the dusty empty barn. He had even danced a little around his invention.

He slipped one dirty finger through the hog wire and tried to jiggle the latch. It was firm. He tried the other side. It was caught firmly too. And the only way to open them, he remembered, was with the blade of a knife. You slipped the knife in and flipped up the latch.

"Piece of cake," he had cried when he flipped them open, a hundred years ago, back in the Blossom barn.

The knife was back at the barn, too, lying on the ground beside the screwdriver.

Junior glanced at his watch: 3:05. Junior shook his head. He guessed that he had been in the trap about twenty-five hours. Tears filled his eyes.

Actually it had only been six minutes, time enough to realize that he was not going to get out of the trap without outside help.

He spent the next six minutes yelling "Help! Will somebody please let me out of this thing! Please!" at the top of his lungs.

He spent the next two minutes listening for sounds of help on the way.

He spent the next two minutes weeping, bent over his knees, his tears rolling down his dusty legs.

A bee buzzed in from the blackberry bushes, and Junior batted it away. "Haven't I got enough trouble without you?" he sobbed.

Chapter Nine
Not a Very Good Coyote

Junior heard a noise. His head snapped up. His swollen eyelids opened.

He swirled around, prepared to meet the glint of wild, golden coyote eyes. For the first time the cage wasn't such a terrible place to be.

There was really only one place where the coyote could sneak up on him. The sides and back of the trap were covered with blackberry bushes; only the front faced a clearing.

And just beyond the clearing, standing behind a tree, watching through the low branches, was Mud. Relief flooded Junior's body like cool water. He had completely forgotten about Mud!

"Mud! Good dog! Come here, boy, come here, Mud. Good old Mud."

Mud flexed his legs and shifted his paws in the pine needles. He did not come.

"Mud, come on, boy! It's me—Junior!" His voice was high with fake good spirits and real despair. "I was just kidding back there in the woods when I told you to go home. I'm glad to see you, Mud. Come on, Mud."

Mud did not move.

Junior had a sudden inspiration. His head flew up so fast, it struck the ceiling of the trap. He didn't stop to rub it. He reached for the tin-can sandwich. He didn't have to bother about being careful with it now. He dangled it from the string like a yo-yo.

"You want some hamburger, Mud? You want some of this?" He waved it in the air to entice Mud. He said, "Hum-hum, is it good. Remember?"

He pinched off a piece, stuck it on the end of one finger, and poked it through the hog wire.

"Look, Mud. Look what I've got. You want some?"

He beckoned to Mud with the finger, luring him closer.

Mud's tail had started to wag. It was sweeping pine needles right and left.

"You do? Well, come on over. Come on, Mud. Good dog!"

Mud got up. Slowly he came across the clearing. He kept his eyes on the ball of hamburger meat, but he was not happy about himself. This whole trip with Junior had been wrong. As soon as he got over feeling bad about one thing, there was something else to feel bad about.

"Come on, Mud!" Junior tried to speed him along by putting extra enthusiasm in his voice. "Come on!"

Mud continued to walk in his slow, ashamed way, his eyes on the ball of pink meat stuck on the end of Ju-

40

nior's finger. Not until he was there, at the hog wire, did he lift his head.

"Sée?" Junior said. Junior allowed Mud to eat the meat from his finger, to lick his fingernail.

"Did you like that? Was it good? Want some more?"

Junior's plan was to get Mud right up against the hog wire and to grab him by the bandanna. Then he would hold Mud so tight that Mud would begin to howl. Mud always howled when he was held tight. "Don't hold the dog," Pap was always saying. "The dog's like me—he don't want to be held!"

So Junior would hold and Mud would howl—and Mud howled like something out of a horror movie. *Ahwooo-ooo-ooooo-ooooo.* It would raise goose bumps on your arms if you didn't know it was just a dog. Mud would howl, and somebody would hear him, and somebody would come.

Mud's soft tongue licked Junior's finger one last time. Junior had a hard time not trying to go for the bandanna right then. He decided to wait. He said calmly, "You want another piece. Here you go."

He dug out another piece with one finger. This time Junior held it inside the hog wire. Mud could reach it with his tongue, and while he was reaching . . . that would be the time to . . . The tone of Junior's voice had made Mud suspicious. He backed away.

"Don't you want it?"

Junior got a bigger piece. "I'm not going to do anything to you," Junior said. "I'm not going to do anything even if it is your fault that I'm in here. If you hadn't poked your nose on my leg and scared me— Anyway,

41

what can I do? Look at me. I'm locked up in a cage. Come on. I just want you to have this nice piece of meat. I know you like it."

Mud came forward. This time he stopped just out of Junior's reach. There was a long moment while Junior held the meat and Mud looked at it. Junior held it closer.

Mud came closer, but something told him not to go too close. He stretched out his neck.

"Here you go, good dog!"

Junior's fingers curved back toward the cage, bringing the meat away from the wire. His other hand was there, the fingers locked in the hog wire, waiting. His fingers flexed, ready to grab the bandanna when the opportunity came.

"Don't you want it?" Junior asked. Sweat was rolling down his face. His tongue flicked over his dry lips. "Take it!"

He had the ball of meat between his fingers now, scissorslike. He beckoned Mud closer.

Mud came.

This was the moment, the opportunity Junior had been waiting for. His fingers hooked into the bandanna, and he pulled Mud hard against the cage.

Mud bucked like a horse. He twisted and pulled and yelped. He threw himself into the air. He tried to duck under the collar and slip his head out.

Junior held on tight. Finally Mud stopped fighting and rested against the cage. His wild eyes were rolled in Junior's direction.

"See, now you just have to howl until somebody

comes," Junior said. He was out of breath from excitement. He tried to swallow, but his throat was too dry.

Beneath his fingers he could feel Mud trembling. "I'm sorry," he gasped. "But I can't let you go yet."

Mud began to whine.

Good, Junior thought. Mud always whined a little before he howled.

Junior's fingers were beginning to hurt. The wire was cutting them. He switched fingers very carefully. Then those fingers began to hurt.

Junior got the inspiration of his life. He would tie the bandanna to the cage. The ends were just long enough. He would take the ends of the bandanna and slip them through the hog wire and knot them.

Getting the ends through the hog wire was easy, but he was having a hard time tying the knot with one hand. Maybe he could let go of the bandanna just long enough to take the ends. There, it worked. Junior had one end of the bandanna in each hand. He bent to make the knot.

At that moment Mud flung himself back so hard that the cage rocked. Junior thought it was going to topple. He let go just long enough to keep from hitting his head.

The next thing Junior saw was Mud's tail disappearing into the woods.

"Come back, come back!" he cried. But Junior knew Mud would not return. He gave one final plea: "Mud, at least show them where I am." But he didn't think Mud would do that either.

Mud was gone for good, and Junior cried for an hour

43

with helpless frustration. At the peak of his misery he rocked back and forth, hitting his head against the cage and not even feeling it. Then he stopped for a while, then he cried again.

The afternoon dragged on. Bees droned in and out of the cage. The sun beat down on his head. His eyes were so swollen from all the crying that he could hardly see. His nose had somehow swollen, too, inside, so he had to breathe through his mouth.

Finally, to ease the pain in his crooked back, he curled up in a small ball. As he lay there on the hard wood, he realized he was nothing like that coyote on Saturday-morning cartoons. That coyote was always ending up the victim of his own traps, too, but then he got right back out.

The unfairness of it brought new tears of misery to his swollen eyes.

I—, he thought—this was his last unhappy thought before he slept—*I don't make a very good coyote.*

Chapter Ten

The Search for Junior

🌿 🌿 🌿

THE BLOSSOMS WERE ON THE FRONT PORCH OF THE house. Vicki Blossom was giving orders. Pap, Vern, Maggie, and Mud were taking them. Supper was over, and the search for Junior was about to get under way.

Overhead, thunder rolled again in the western sky. This time the sound was louder. The storm was coming closer.

"All right now, what we're looking for is wheelbarrow tracks. If we can follow those, we'll find Junior. There's about—" She broke off and looked up at the threatening sky. "There's about three hours before night. We've got to find Junior before then."

She looked at them, one by one, as if to impress on each one the seriousness of the situation. They didn't need her looks to tell them that. Since supper an uneasy feeling had come over all of them. This was not one of Junior's usual absences. This time Junior was absent— each one knew this—because he could not help being absent. Something had happened to Junior.

45

Pap was the only one who spoke. "I sure do hate it when somebody's missing." He shook his head slowly, back and forth. "It leaves a hole."

In the silence that followed, Mud moved closer to Pap and leaned against his leg. Pap stepped aside, catching Mud off balance.

Mud straightened and looked longingly at Pap. He had the feeling that there was an enormous distance between him and Pap instead of the few inches that actually separated them.

Ever since Pap had come home from can collecting and said, "Well, where were you when I needed you?" in a certain accusing tone, Mud had known he was out of favor. It was the first can collection he had ever missed.

"Go on, I don't want to pet you." Pap had gone into the house and shut the door in Mud's face.

"I'll pet you, Mud," Maggie had said, but Maggie's hugs only made him struggle harder to get to the screen door so he could scratch on it and follow Pap inside.

And even after Maggie let him in, all Pap said was "I said I don't want to pet you."

Mud could not bear being out of favor with Pap. In the past hour he had done everything he could to make up to Pap for his desertion.

First he had pushed his head into Pap's hand, giving Pap the chance to scratch his nose. Pap had not. Then he had poked his head under Pap's hand. Pap's hand had been like a cap on his head for a brief, satisfactory moment, and then Pap had moved it. Then Mud had rested his chin on Pap's leg during supper. Pap had shrugged him off. Now Mud moved closer to Pap for another try at leaning against his leg. Pap said, "Let's go."

Pap went down the steps so heavily, the boards bowed beneath his weight. Mud went behind him, staying close, hoping to hear Pap speak his name or touch him in the old pal-to-pal way.

The five of them followed the wheelbarrow tracks into the woods. Junior had taken a curving, weaving route, skirting trees and large rocks. It was easy to follow because Junior had been in a hurry and had torn up the moss and pine needles.

"Junior!" Vicki called. "Oh, Junior!"

No answer.

They tracked him through the creek. The wheel had been stuck briefly in the mud. It had apparently taken Junior three separate tries to get it up the bank.

"Junior! Oh, Junior!"

Still no answer.

At the edge of the old wheat field they ran into trouble. The ground was hard, and the old wheat so broken, they couldn't find a single mark.

"Here's where we split up," Vicki said. "Fan out and if you see anything, holler!"

With their eyes on the ground they proceeded slowly across the old field. Every now and then Vicki would pause to call Junior and to say in a worried way, "He ought to be able to hear me by now. Why doesn't he answer?"

"Now, Vicki," Pap would answer from across the

rows of stubble. To calm himself he muttered, "We'll find him. We'll find him."

"Here's the track! He went this way!" Pap called suddenly. Being the one to spot the wheelbarrow tracks, particularly after a long time of looking, gave Pap a good feeling. "Over here!" he called. Pap's voice sounded so good that Mud bounded over the wheat field to him.

"Come on, Mud, let's find him," Pap said. He reached out with one hand and brushed Mud's head.

Mud happily took the lead. As he bounded to the woods his tail began to wag.

Chapter Eleven
Mad Mary's Find

✤ ✤ ✤

MAD MARY STOPPED WITH HER HAND REACHING FOR some low blackberries. Her hand dropped to her knee.

"Well, look at that. Somebody put a little child in a cage."

She knelt. Her ragged skirts flared out around her. Mad Mary had not changed her clothes in five years. When one skirt wore out, she just put another one on top of it. She had layers of rags now, some so old and colorless, even she did not know what the cloth had once looked like.

As she bent forward, her boots dug into the dust Junior had piled against the trap. Her socks bagged around her thin white ankles. She leaned her weight against her cane.

She watched Junior's curled figure for a moment, shaking her head, making little clicking sounds with her mouth. *Tsk, tsk, tsk.* It was the sound she used to make a lot when she was living around people. She made it every time she saw an example of man's cruelty to his fellow man. Since she had started living by herself, she had not had to make the sound one single time.

Junior lay on his side. His thumb was beneath his chin, as if it had just fallen out of his mouth. His eyes were red and swollen. When he breathed in and out, unspilled tears rattled in his throat.

Mad Mary reached out her freckled hand and unlocked one latch, then the other. She didn't need a knife blade. Her fingernails were long, tough, and sharp. She could puncture a can of condensed milk with them.

She lifted the door silently and got it out of the way by tying it to the tree limb overhead. She knotted the fishing line with one hand, without looking up.

She brushed a bee aside as if it were a fly.

"Now let's get you out of here before whoever done this to you comes back," she said.

She leaned in the trap and, with surprising gentleness, pulled Junior toward her. He did not stir. She scooped him into her arms.

Junior was so worn out with trying to get free and with crying and with the pain of being a caged animal that he felt nothing. If this was what it was like to be in a trap—he had thought this at least a hundred times during the endless afternoon—if this was what it was like, he would never make another trap as long as he lived.

Mad Mary braced him against her knee for a moment and then lifted him. Years of living on her own in the woods had made her strong. Nothing bothered her. As she stood, Junior's head rolled into a comfortable curve of her shoulder.

50

"There you go," she said.

He moaned.

"You sleep," she told him.

She adjusted him so she would have the use of her walking cane. She needed that. The cane poked into the dust, leaving a sharp indentation by her feet.

"When you wake up, all your bad dreams will be over. You'll be safe. Nobody can get you in Mary's cave. Nobody even knows where Mary's cave is."

With long mannish strides Mad Mary bore Junior away deeper into the forest.

"And that," she said to the trees and the storm breeze and the darkening sky, "is a fact."

Mud was running wildly through the trees. His long ears flared out behind him. Now he remembered Junior in the bushes. He remembered the hamburger. He knew exactly where they were going and why.

He turned, barked over his shoulder, and then ran back in a frenzy to make sure the Blossoms were following him. He barked again to speed them up and then ran deeper into the woods.

"Mud knows something," Pap said, panting.

"Sure! He was with Junior!" Vern called over his shoulder.

"That's right! He was, Pap!"

At that, Maggie began running faster. She caught up with Vern and they ran together like forest creatures, jumping over briar bushes, slipping through the narrow spaces between trees, sliding down banks.

Their mom tried to keep up with them for a while,

but she had to fall back when she lost one of her Dr. Scholl's sandals. She slid her foot in again and ran forward, calling, "We're coming, Junior!"

Behind them, Pap could not keep up no matter how hard he tried. He was thrashing through the forest like a wounded moose. He was desperately trying to catch the others, but it was impossible. He watched them disappear, one by one, into the trees. His sense of frustration deepened.

The forest itself seemed to be fighting him. He pushed aside branches and they came back to slap him in the face. Briars caught his clothes and tore them. His shoelace got busted, and a loose stone turned his ankle onto its side.

"Wait for me!" he called, staggering to a stop. No one even heard him.

Pap tested his throbbing ankle by walking three steps to a tree. He held on to the tree as if it were his last friend. Then, as he leaned there, he suddenly felt old and useless. He put his weight on the tree.

Above his own ragged breathing he could hear Mud's joyful barking in the distance. It seemed to be in one place now. Mud had found Junior.

Well, that was good. Pap imagined Vern and Maggie and Vicki catching up. He imagined them running into the clearing, hugging each other, being happy and young. He wished he could be there.

It's terrible being old, he thought, terrible. His despair returned. He put his hand on his hip for support and bent his knees. He was going to sit down on a stone.

Suddenly in the distance he heard Vicki's voice. She

was calling him. "Pap!" she cried. It was the voice she used when something bad had happened, the voice she had used on the phone the night she'd called to tell him his son, Cotton, had been killed by a steer. He had heard that cry enough to know it in his sleep. Her saying his name in that way turned his blood cold every time.

Pap's knees were bent so he could sit down, and it was hard for him to get his knees to realize they were going to have to straighten up instead and take him on through the forest.

He gave each knee a gentle nudge with his fist, and they popped back. He began his awkward push through the forest, favoring his bad ankle.

"I'm coming," he called, hobbling toward them. "I'm coming."

Chapter Twelve
The Cage

❧ ❧ ❧

PAP CAME INTO THE CLEARING WITH ONE HAND OVER his pounding heart. "What?" he gasped. "What's happened?"

Vicki pointed to the cage set back in the blackberry bushes. Pap stumbled forward. He squinted. His hand clutched the bib of his overalls.

"What?" he said again. He didn't see anything, so he guessed he must not be looking in the right place. His head snapped this way and that. His neck bones creaked in protest.

"There, Pap," Maggie said. She pointed too.

"I don't see nothing."

"Exactly!" Vicki Blossom's voice wavered with tears. "Junior's gone. There is the cage and Junior's gone!"

Pap walked forward slowly. Now he could see the cage, the blackberry branches twined carefully into the hog wire, the trapdoor pulled up and tied to an overhead limb, the dirt pulled onto the wood floor to give the appearance of earth. The dirt had been scraped off in places as if something had been dragged through it.

Pap still couldn't take it in. He stood, his body shaking beneath his worn overalls—the trembles, he called it. He got the trembles when he got cold or sick or when the world got to be too much for him.

"I don't get it," he said helplessly.

Vern was used to explaining things to Pap. "Pap, Junior set the trap, see, but something or somebody sprung it. See, I figured it out. The bait was right here between these can tops. The string was stuck inside. There, like that. And see"—he pointed overhead—"Junior never tied that knot. I know Junior's knots. He would have worked it like this."

Deftly Vern began to untie the fishing line. He restrung it, leaned in the trap, and reset it. "There. That's the way Junior would have set it up. I know Junior's work." He faced the still-bewildered Pap.

Vicki Blossom snorted with impatience and turned her back on all of them.

"The main thing, Pap," Vern went on patiently, "is that Junior would not have tied that knot and Junior would never, ever have left the wheelbarrow." Vern pointed to the overturned wheelbarrow beside the trap.

"Well, could be he went home, could be we passed him in the woods."

"Not with me calling him every step of the way," Vicki said.

"And not without taking the wheelbarrow." That, to Vern, was the scariest thing. "That's your wheelbarrow, Pap, we gave it to you for Christmas. Junior would never have gone off and left it unless he couldn't help himself." They all knew this was true. Junior had chipped in hard-earned cash so his name could be on the card, and for that reason the wheelbarrow was especially valuable to him.

"Let me think a minute," Pap said. He closed his eyes and rubbed his dusty brow.

"I'm tired of everybody standing around thinking. Thinking never got anybody anywhere. We need to do something."

"I know that."

"This is all we need to know. He came out here to set the trap, right? And somehow after he set it, he—" His mother turned her back again. She could not bring herself to say the word *disappeared.*

"Junior knows these woods," Pap said, stubbornly refusing to admit the possibility of disaster. "He knew how to get here, didn't he? We've come blackberry picking enough times—and so he knew how to get home. The boy ain't dumb."

"I know that, Pap, but accidents happen to people all the time, real smart people. You don't have to be dumb to have something terrible—" Maggie broke off. "It could even be a kidnapping." Tears came to her eyes at the thought. The grocery store where they bought milk had pictures of missing children on the cartons, and the thought of Junior's face on one was too painful even to imagine.

Pap had the trembles so bad now, his whole body was shaking. "What do you want me to do?"

"I want you to tell us what to do!" Vicki said. Panic caused her voice to rise.

57

Thunder rumbled overhead now. Dark clouds covered the sky. The afternoon had been absolutely still, but now a storm breeze began to blow.

"Well, let's do something even if it's wrong."

"All right, Pap, but what?"

"Let me think." There was a long pause. Mud was at Pap's feet, looking up at him.

For ten minutes Mud had been waiting for his praise, the words *Good dog,* but the words had not come. He had found the place—that's obviously what they were looking for, this place—and yet no one had praised him. No one even seemed to know he was there.

He gave one faint bark, deep in his throat, to get Pap's attention, but Pap did not look down. His body just kept shaking in a way that made Mud uneasy.

"Let's go back to the house," Pap said. He paused and swallowed. The next words were hard to say. "And call the police."

Chapter Thirteen

The Cave

LIGHTNING WAS STREAKING THE SKY WHEN MAD Mary started up the slope to her cave. The wind was whipping the trees, and the pale underside of the ash leaves flickered among the darker green of the firs.

"We'll get there before the storm hits," she told the exhausted, sleeping boy in her arms. "Don't you worry about that."

It had been a long walk, deep into the woods where nobody except an occasional hunter came. They had moved without stopping, over the long grassless stretch where nothing would grow, the old people said, because of Indian graves underneath. They had paused to rest at the old quarry by the pool of still green water. Junior never stirred. They crossed two creeks and waded through ferns high enough to brush Junior's back. They rested again at the foot of Owl Hill in laurel so thick, it was like stepping into twilight. They rested again at the foot of Castle Rock.

All the while the sky overhead grew darker, and the

rumble of thunder came closer. Lightning flashed more often in the leaden clouds.

Finally, at the foot of a craggy hill, Mad Mary paused. She was used to climbing this uneven hill, as most people are used to climbing their own stairways. Indeed the fallen limestone formed something like steps. But Mad Mary had never gone up with so heavy a burden as Junior.

She felt for her footing. She couldn't see the ground because of Junior, but finally she felt a limestone rock she knew.

"Oh, we'll be all right," she said. She started up. She was surefooted now, and a crack of lightning lit up the path. She knew the storm was about to break.

Mad Mary lived almost at the top of Vulture Roost. It was an outcropping of rocks a flock of vultures had called home for as long as anyone could remember. In past years there had been thirty or more; now there were only six. And those six vultures were hidden in the high rocks, sheltered from the coming storm.

Beneath the limestone peaks was a cave. It wasn't a cave with beautiful dripping rocks and interesting formations and passages. There was nothing to tempt explorers. It was just a big hollow comfortable space in the rocks. Nobody had come to this cave in years.

At the entrance was a ledge, and here the laurel grew so thick that from below, the cave couldn't be seen at all. Mad Mary paused there on the ledge to get her breath. Junior sagged in her tired arms.

She turned and glanced at the sky. It was black as

night now. "Rain, if you want to," she told it. "Go ahead. I'm home. Rain!"

The wind blew. It picked up, whipping her skirts around her thin legs. And, as if on signal, the first drops of rain began to splatter against the limestone rocks. They left wet spots as big as quarters.

Mad Mary shouldered the laurel aside and ducked into the cave with Junior clutched tightly in her arms.

Chapter Fourteen
Dust Marks the Spot

ᘓᶠ   ᘓᶠ   ᘓᶠ

"WAIT A MINUTE."

"What?"

Vern had dropped to his knees in the dust and was looking intently at the ground.

"What?" Vicki Blossom asked again. Her voice seemed more strained every time she spoke.

"Those aren't Junior's footprints."

"Where?"

Vern pointed with the finger he had once blown half off with a stray dynamite cap. "Those are not Junior's footprints!"

Together the Blossoms drew close to look at the broad-toed prints in the dust. Junior had piled the dust against the cage and also inside it to disguise it. He had patted the dust smooth. The faint print of his fingers was still there, around the deep footprints.

Maggie said, "Junior had on tennis shoes. These look like boots."

"Man's boots," Vern said.

"Maybe," Pap said.

There was something in the way Pap said that one word that got their attention. Vicki Blossom looked up, squinting. She was kneeling by the prints so she could see them better. "What do you mean, Pap? Do you know something?"

With his toe Pap pointed to another mark in the dust.

"What is that, Pap?"

She bent closer, her hair falling over her face. Maggie was on her knees, too, her braids sweeping the dust. Only Pap stood erect. If he got down, he'd never get up.

From his height he said, "Cane mark."

"Cane? You mean a man with a cane . . ." Vicki paused in confusion. "You mean some man with a cane was here? Who? What man?"

"It ain't only men that wear men's boots. It ain't only men that carry canes."

"Pap, if you know something, tell me!"

"Not a man," Pap said. "A woman."

"A woman?"

Pap swallowed. He had the trembles so bad now that he stuffed his hands in the bib of his overalls to keep them from fluttering.

Maggie and Vern breathed in at the same time. When they breathed out, they said the name for him:

"Mad Mary."

"Mad Mary? That old woman that goes around eating animals off the road. She's got Junior? You can't be serious! The woman really is mad!" Vicki said.

"She won't hurt Junior," Pap said.

"Then why did she take him?"

Pap shook his head slowly, from side to side. "That's what I don't know."

Mad Mary loved a good storm. It was the time she felt safest and happiest in her cave.

The rest of the world was out there worrying about electricity going out and lightning striking and leaks in the roof and wind damage. Mad Mary didn't have to worry about one single thing.

Mad Mary drew on her pipe. She had filled it with wild tobacco.

She leaned back in her rocking chair. This rocking chair was the only stick of real furniture she had, the only furniture she needed. At night she rocked in it before the fire. On sunny days she pulled it out on the ledge and rocked out there. On cold and stormy nights she pulled a quilt on her lap for comfort.

On the fire in front of her simmered the rabbit, the squirrel, and the onions. She had thrown in a potato and two carrots too. She bent forward from time to time and stirred the bubbling mixture with a handmade spoon.

The light from the fire played on the cave walls. The flickering shadows magnified the bunches of herbs drying on the walls, and made the corners deep and foreboding.

Junior groaned in his sleep, and Mad Mary glanced over at the ledge where he lay. The noise startled her for a moment. She had forgotten he was there.

He moved—he was under a quilt too—but he did not wake up.

64

"You sleep. You're safe," she said. Smoke curled around her pipe.

Junior had turned over and was now facing Mad Mary. One arm was flung out of the covers, in her direction, as if he were asking for something.

The lightning flashed, lighting up his features, turning them white. Mad Mary waited to see if the lightning would wake him, but it didn't.

"I never saw a child that worn out." She shook her head, remembering the cruel condition in which she had found him. "Poor little thing. Maybe I ought to wake him up for supper. He's probably starved. They never left him anything to eat but some raw hamburger."

She hesitated. "No," she said finally, "he probably needs sleep as much as anything."

Then she bent over her stew. Wonderful-smelling steam misted her face. It was done. She began spooning it out, ladling it onto an old pie tin. She balanced the pie tin on her quilt-covered lap and began to eat.

Outside, the rain poured and the thunder rumbled. Mad Mary forgot the storm. Mad Mary forgot Junior. By the flickering firelight she ate her varmint stew.

Chapter Fifteen
Left Behind

🌿ˣ 🌿ˣ 🌿ˣ

"I WANTED TO GO WITH THEM."

"You didn't want to go any worse than me."

"Yeah, but you have a hurt ankle, Pap," Maggie said. "You couldn't go."

"Oh, yes I could," Pap said, his chin jutting out stubbornly.

Maggie and Pap were sitting on the front porch, in the swing, waiting for the police. All they had been talking about was how much they had wanted to go with Vern and Vicki on the search for Mad Mary's place. Both of them wanted to be where the action was.

By turns, they pushed the swing back and forth, back and forth.

"I was the logical one to go," Pap said, "because I went to school with the woman. I knowed her. We was in a talent show one time in grade school."

Maggie was so startled, she stopped the swing. It bobbed awkwardly on its chains.

"Pap, you and Mad Mary were in a talent show?"

"My talent, naturally, was rope tricks," he went on.

That talent show was one of Pap's favorite childhood memories. For a long time he had even had a picture of himself in the western costume his mama had put together for the talent show. He wished he still had it. He remembered himself as looking like Will Rogers.

Maggie looked at him. She was having a hard time bringing the picture into focus. Finally she said, "I can see you doing rope tricks, but what on earth was Mad Mary's talent?"

"Singing. Everybody said she got to sing because her daddy owned the mill. Folks were jealous of the Cantrells back then, because of their money, but as I remember it, she done all right. I remember she wore a yellow dress, and her mother was the only lady there that had on gloves and a hat."

"Mad Mary sang, Pap?" Maggie still couldn't take it in.

"High."

She shook her head in amazement. "Were you friends with her, Pap?"

"I don't reckon you'd call us friends. We sat side by side in school for three years. They done it alphabetically back then, and Blossom came right before Cantrell. In fifth grade Dickie Lee Bunker skipped a grade, and from then on he sat between us."

He shook his head. "No, we wasn't friends, but she was as much my friend as anybody's. The Cantrells always did keep to themselves. Anyway, she knows me. One time—oh, this was after the Cantrell family place burned and Mary made a shed out of the ruins. She was the talk of the town back then."

"She still is."

Pap ignored Maggie's comment.

"The place burned down and Mr. Cantrell with it," he went on, "and for some reason Mary wouldn't leave and come into town like a normal person. Nobody could talk any sense to her. She just kept poking around in the ruins and dragging out a shutter here, a door there. The week after her father's funeral she started dragging the stuff down to the river—boards, bricks, you name it. She made the whole shed by herself. She always was strong, both in will and body."

It was Pap's turn to set the swing in motion.

"Well, anyway, this particular day I saw Mary in the grocery store. We was reaching for the same can of Carnation milk. We excused ourselves and then she looked at me close and said, 'Weren't you the little skinny boy who was always doing rope tricks?'

"I said, 'Yes, ma'am, and didn't you used to sing Ave Maria?' "

Pap stuck his chin out again. "That's why I ought to be the one going to hunt for her. She'd remember me. I wouldn't startle her. Them she won't know from strangers, might bolt like a scared animal and carry Junior halfway to Blowing Rock."

Pap scratched his unshaved chin. The whiskers grated against his fingers.

"No, Mary never was one to cotton to strangers."

Chapter Sixteen

The Mud Trap

🌿 🌿 🌿

MUD WAS SITTING BY JUNIOR'S COYOTE TRAP. HE WAS torn between following Pap and Maggie to the house or going with Vickie and Vern on their trip into the woods.

Normally there wouldn't have been any question about the matter. He would have gone with Pap. But the last thing Pap had said to him was "Go with Vern." He had pointed it out for him so there would be no mistake. "The dog might be some help to you, Vicki."

"All right. I'll take him with us. Now, Pap, you call the police as soon as you get home. Maggie, you make sure he does."

"I will." Maggie kicked the dust. "But I still don't see why I can't come with you."

"I told you, shug. I need you to go with Pap."

When her mom called her shug, Maggie always obeyed. She got in one final "But I still don't see why."

Mud sat listening to this in front of the coyote trap. The people had lost interest in him, and Pap and Maggie had already started across the clearing. Pap was pushing the wheelbarrow.

"Come on, Mud," Vern called. He snapped his fingers twice.

Mud got up and stretched. He lifted his leg in the direction of the coyote cage, and then abruptly he lowered it.

Mud smelled hamburger. He sniffed the ground. The smell seemed to be coming from inside the cage. He walked slowly toward it. With his head lowered he paused and sniffed again.

"Come on, Mud," Vern's voice called. The voice was fading into the distance. Vern and Vicki were already out of sight. Maggie and Pap were too.

Mud's nose began to run. He could see that at the back of the trap lay a large piece of hamburger meat. It was under a piece of metal. Mud hesitated, then he lowered his head and crawled into the cage.

Although the cage was taller than he was, something told Mud to move in a crouch. When he was halfway inside, he tried to scrape the metal toward him with one paw. His sharp toenails left scratches in the dust.

He couldn't reach it. He crawled all the way in. He pawed the metal circle.

And this time, he could reach it. The tin-can sandwich flipped over like a tiddlywink. Before Mud could take it in his mouth, however, there was a terrible whooshing noise behind him. Leaves and dust and blackberries and bugs flew into the air. Then there were two clicking noises, and silence.

Mud had darted back in fear, but he found he was up against a door. He tried to dart the other way. Wire. He leapt up in alarm. He struck his head on the roof of the cage. He spent the next minutes twisting desperately this way and that, hitting boards or wire wherever he turned.

His yellow eyes grew wild. He panted with fear.

For the second time that day Junior's coyote trap had made a catch.

Hello, Mud.

"Well, at last," Pap said, getting to his feet. "Here come the police. Perfect timing," he added scornfully, "here comes the rain too."

"I like the police," Maggie said, remembering the events of the Blossoms' last July. "They sure helped us last summer."

"I ain't said nothing against them. Just their timing," Pap said.

The police car stopped at the porch. A policeman opened the front door and ducked as if he were trying to get under the rain. He ran for the porch. The other policeman followed with one hand steadying his gun.

"You took your time," Pap commented.

"We got here as fast as we could, sir."

"Well, let's go in the house and sit down," Pap said. "We've got some trouble to tell you about." He held the door open. "You boys know who Mary Cantrell is, don't you?"

"Would that be Mad Mary?" the policeman asked.

"It would," Maggie said, and she followed the policemen into the house.

Chapter Seventeen

In the Cave

JUNIOR AWOKE.

For a minute he thought his eyes were still closed. He was in absolute, total blackness. He had never seen anything like it. He touched his face, felt the slits in his swollen eyelids.

No, his eyes were open. But he couldn't see a thing. How could this be happening? He choked with sudden fear. He was blind!

A moan began deep in his chest. His hands groped on either side of his body. He felt nothing familiar, nothing he had ever felt before. What was this? And this?

Rags!

He was lying in a bed of rags. His hands fumbled over the cloth. Not rags, old blankets. His fear grew. These were not like any old blankets he had ever felt before. And beneath the unknown blankets was— He drew in another ragged breath.

Stone!

He was lying on stone! The feel of the cold, hard stone

73

made Junior stop breathing entirely. His hands trembled over the stone to see where it ended. It didn't. The wall was stone too.

The discovery left him petrified. He could not move. When at last he began to breathe again, he noticed for the first time how different the air was. Junior had never breathed air like this before. And there was a strange, foreign smell in the cold air. A smell of old smoke and cooking, but even the cooking smell wasn't familiar.

Where was he? His hands moved over his body to see if that was still the same. It was, but he was under a cover, a quilt. It was ragged, too, and it smelled musty. Junior threw it away with a strangled cry.

He staggered to his feet. He had begun to really cry now, but it was such a new sort of crying, he didn't even recognize it as his. It was the wail of a lost, hurt animal. He stretched out his arms and began to stumble blindly across the uneven floor.

At once he tripped and fell forward. His face struck stone. His front teeth went through his lip. He tasted blood.

Junior screamed. The scream echoed in the still cold air, and the sound of his amplified scream scared Junior so much, he screamed again.

He began to crawl forward on his stomach, moving in desperation, screaming as he went, wiggling from side to side like a lizard. Suddenly his hand touched something that felt familiar.

His scream caught in his throat. His hand moved over the new object.

74

A shoe!

Junior wanted to cry, this time with relief. Where there was a shoe, there had to be a person. This was the first time Junior could believe he might still be in the real world. His hand moved up. It was a boot. Shoelaces.

Then his trembling hand recognized the top of a sock. And above that, the rough skin of a leg.

"Pap?"

Suddenly a kitchen match flared above him, and Junior looked up. He saw a sight he would never forget for the rest of his life. It was a Halloween mask come to life.

The blood rushed from his head so fast, his face turned white as paper. His eyes rolled up into his head. A voice far, far away said, "It's just me."

Junior saw no more and heard no more. For the first time in his life Junior fainted.

Chapter Eighteen

Howling in the Rain

✣ ✣ ✣

THE COYOTE TRAP WAS A MISERABLE PLACE TO BE after the storm began.

At first Mud kept getting up and shaking himself. He never had liked the feel of rain dripping through his fur. Then he would curl back into a mound. Then the rain dripping through his fur would get on his nerves again and he would get up and shake.

But after a while his yellow fur was so soaked, he looked brown. About that time Mud gave up on getting dry and crouched as far back in the trap as he could get. His golden eyes were dark with misery.

In the wood floor of the cage were deep gashes, the results of ninety minutes of Mud's digging. Mud was a good digger, and there was nothing he could not dig his way out of—nothing but this coyote trap. He had dug so long and so hard, his front paws were bloody.

Since the rain had begun, there had not been one single thing to give Mud hope—not the sound of a footstep, not the sound of a voice; there had been nothing but rain and thunder and lightning, three things Mud had dreaded since, as a puppy, he had cringed with his mother, Minnie, under the porch during storms.

Minnie's shivers and shuddering sighs had taught Mud more than enough about thunderstorms.

About dark, Mud threw back his head and began to howl. He was a strong howler—he got that from his mom too—and tonight he was miserable enough to be in good voice. *Awhoooo-oo-ooooo! Awhoooooooo-oo-ooooo!*

But if anybody had heard him, they would have thought it was only the wind.

"Vern, we are going to have to turn back!" Vicki shouted over the noise of the storm.

Vern blinked the rain out of his eyes.

"We can't even see where we're going."

"Mom, we have to keep looking!"

"We're going around in circles."

"Mom!"

For a while Vern and Vicki Blossom had been able to follow Mad Mary's trail by her footprints and, especially, the marks of her cane. They seemed to be calling "Here's one!" all the time. Since the rain had started, they hadn't found anything.

"Mom, we can't give up!"

Vern was wet, cold, hungry, and miserable. As he made his way through the woods, the one thing that kept him going was the memory of Mad Mary. Every time Vern had seen her, even if it was in a public place, like on a highway, a scared feeling had come over him.

He didn't understand it. It wasn't just ordinary fear. He was afraid of a lot of people. This was more like dread, a sick dread, to be exact.

And now Mad Mary, the woman he himself dreaded so much—that woman had Junior.

"We can't give up! We can't."

His mom put her arm around him. The lightning flashed, turned the world white. She hugged him harder than he could remember ever being hugged in his whole life. Then she said, "Come on, we're going home."

Tears began running down Vern's cheeks, along with the rain. "You go on," he said.

"We're going home."

Finally he allowed himself to be turned around. With his mom's arm around his shoulders he started walking. Every time he slowed down, his mom's arm would tighten around his shoulder.

There was another flash of lightning. A tree had been hit. Limbs crashed to the ground just behind them.

Vicki screamed. "Run!"

She dropped her arm from around him, and they both broke into a run for home.

"I knowed they wouldn't do nothing."

"They can't do anything, Pap, in the storm."

"They could. They just don't want to get wet."

"Oh, Pap."

"They don't," Pap said stubbornly. "They have to pay for their own dry cleaning."

This time Maggie's answer was a sigh.

78

"What's wrong with you?" Pap asked.

"I can't stand to wait, Pap. For one solid hour we waited for the police, and now it's been another hour waiting for Mom and Vern. I can't stand to wait!"

"You get that from my side of the family," Pap said mildly.

"I want to be part of every single thing that happens in the world, not waiting for it."

"I never wanted to be part of every single thing," Pap said carefully. "These days there's lots you're better off being out of."

"I like action."

"Maybe I'm just getting too old for action. Action ain't what it used to be."

Maggie and Pap were now sitting in the living room because the storm was blowing so hard. Sheets of rain were sweeping across the yard, and Pap had gone in the kitchen twice for pots to put under the leaks. Over the sound of the driving rain was the steady *ker-plunk* of drips falling into cooking pots.

This time it was Pap who sighed, and Maggie who asked "What's wrong?"

"Same old thing. I just want everybody to be home. We Blossoms sure have a time staying together."

"That's right," Maggie said, "we sure do."

Chapter Nineteen

By Dawn's Early Light

JUNIOR AWOKE AT DAWN. HE HAD JUST HAD THE worst nightmare of his life.

In the nightmare Junior was lost in a grocery store. Everybody in the store looked like his mom from the back, so he kept running up to these ladies and throwing his arms around their legs. These ladies were extremely tall.

Then these ladies would turn around, look down at him, and there, instead of his mom's face, would be the terrible, real-life Halloween face of last night. Junior had only seen that face once, by the light of a kitchen match, but every terrifying feature was etched into his brain.

In the nightmare he would scream and run out of the dairy department and to another mom in frozen foods. There would be another desperate embrace, then the turn, the horrible face, the scream. He woke up running from one mom in pet supplies to another in fresh produce. And by this time the ladies weren't waiting for him to hug them. They would turn and give him that terrifying grin while he was still running toward them!

At first Junior was glad to be awake, then he remembered where he was. Without opening his eyes, he knew he was back on the same ledge, on the same ragged blankets, covered with the same musty quilt, breathing the same chilly air. He shuddered.

A moan almost escaped his lips, but he held it back. He wanted to be asleep—at least to look asleep in case the witch was still there. As long as he was asleep—or looked asleep—the day could not start.

He lay there without moving for what seemed like hours. He was listening. He heard nothing. Finally he cracked one eye.

The light was dim and everything had a gray look. Nothing moved in the sooty distance. Junior opened his other eye. He leaned up on one elbow.

He was so astonished that he sat straight up. He was in a cave. This place was a cave! How could it be? He had fallen asleep in a trap and now . . . now . . . , his brain sputtered, now he was in a cave!

He got to his feet and began to walk around. He was too surprised not to. He paused. A rocking chair. There was a rocking chair in this cave.

There was no end to the surprises. He walked around, touching everything. All Junior's life his family had tried to break him of the habit of touching other people's things—he was so used to having them slap his hand in department stores that he hardly felt it anymore. Now there was nobody to stop him. He touched everything.

A pile of rags and old clothes over here had been covered with a blanket; it was a chair. Another pile of old clothes by the fire was a sort of stool. There were pots and pans and bottles of water lined up on a rock ledge.

Another rock ledge made a table, and there were old dishes on it. And at the back of the ledge there were shelves made out of boards and rocks. On these shelves was food, real grocery store stuff, the same kind of stuff the Blossoms had on their shelves—matches and flour and salt. Junior didn't know witches used matches and flour and salt.

And there were jars of dried apples and strings of peppers and baskets of sprouting potatoes and shriveled carrots. Junior stepped back to see what he'd missed, and he bumped into the cave wall. Something brushed his head.

He looked up, startled. There were all kinds of weeds hanging on the walls. That was more like it. Witchweeds. Junior reached up and touched a bunch.

It was dried and some leaves crumbled in his fingers. He brushed his hand against his pants, and when he lifted his hand, his fingers had a spicy smell. Junior wiped his hand quickly on his pants again.

Junior kept walking. And over there, by the door, were boxes and boxes and more boxes. Junior had never seen so many boxes. He bent down to see the contents.

Books.

He threw back the lid on another box.

More books.

Junior's mouth dropped open in amazement. There were more books in these boxes, in this cave, than in the whole school library.

To Junior these books were the most astonishing thing of all. He had never, ever known of a witch who liked to read.

Chapter Twenty
The Longest Day

🌿   🌿   🌿

THE REST OF THE BLOSSOMS WERE UP AT DAWN TOO. They were in the kitchen, sitting around the table.

"Now, I know nobody's hungry," Vicki Blossom was saying, "but we all got to eat. It may be a long day."

"I hope not," Pap said. "I can't take many more long days."

"Then stay home."

The sharpness of her tone made everybody look up. "I'm sorry," she said. "I did not sleep one wink last night and I am worried sick." She reached for a big spoon and began to serve the oatmeal. She shook raisins on top, but she was so nervous, the raisins rained onto the table.

"I'll do that, Mom." Maggie took the raisin box and finished the job.

"I'm sorry. Please just let me alone. I'll be all right in a minute." She put one hand to her forehead. "Did I call the beauty shop and tell them I wouldn't be in?"

"Yes, Mom."

84

"I can't seem to remember anything." She got up and stood with her back to them. She poured herself another cup of coffee and went to the window to drink it. "Well, one good thing," she said, trying to sound as if she were in control of herself now, "the rain's stopped. The search won't be in the rain."

"What time's the search supposed to start?"

"Seven o'clock."

"I hope there's a lot of people." Vern said. "I don't know where Mad Mary lives, but I bet it's a hundred miles from nowhere."

"Will you please stop calling her that?" Vicki said without turning around.

"What?"

"Mad Mary."

"Sure."

A silence fell over the table then. Maggie was swinging her legs under the table, and she was the first to realize that Mud was not there. She never swung her legs without hitting Mud. Never. She leaned down and looked.

"Where's Mud?"

Pap looked at Vicki's tight, unyielding back and then at Vern. "Didn't he go with you and your mom last night?"

"No."

"I told him to."

"I know, but he didn't. I thought he followed you on back to the house."

"No." Pap sighed and dropped his spoon into his oatmeal. "Now we got two missing Blossoms."

Vicki spun around. "A missing dog is not like a missing child."

Again the fury in her face and voice startled Pap. He pulled back into his overalls to get out of her way. "I know that."

"Well, you don't act like it."

Vicki Blossom threw her coffee mug in the sink. "I'm going out. People ought to be coming soon."

"Mom's really uptight," Maggie said when they heard the screen door slam. She patted Pap's arm. "Having Mud missing isn't the same as having Junior missing. We all know that, but, Pap, Mud is just as much a Blossom as any of us." She got up. "I'm going out too."

Junior pulled back a laurel branch and peered outside. He gasped and stepped back. She was out there!

He flattened himself against the side of the cave and glanced around for somewhere to hide—under some rags maybe; but Junior knew he always trembled when he was scared, and so the rags would tremble too. Maybe behind one of the boxes of books. Maybe he could push two boxes together and—

Breaking off his thoughts, he held his breath and peered through the laurels again.

She was still there. The woman. THE woman. And he didn't have to turn her around to see what her face was like. He had done that enough in his grocery store nightmare.

What was she doing? Why was she just standing there, looking down the hill? Did she see something? Could somebody be coming for him? He would give a hundred million dollars to see her wave, to hear her call "If you're looking for a little boy, he's up here."

Instead she did the thing he most did not want her to do. She turned.

The turn happened so fast that Junior didn't have time to duck back in the cave and dive for the books. He barely had time to cover his eyes so he wouldn't have to see that terrible face again.

A voice said, "Well, come on out."

Junior was too scared to disobey.

With his hands over his eyes, he took one step through the laurels and out into the misty July morning.

Chapter Twenty-one

The Search Party

$\sim$ $\sim$ $\sim$

"THIS ISN'T NEARLY AS MANY PEOPLE AS WE NEED, Pap," Vicki Blossom said.

She and Pap were standing on the porch, looking at the people gathered on the wet lawn.

"I thought when the call went out on both the radio and the television, we'd have hundreds of people."

"Well, we don't," Pap said.

"That is obvious," she said. "Twenty-six people, total."

"Some of them my age."

"And some of them just kids. Look over there. And that boy with the little brothers—he limps worse than you."

"Now, Vicki, that's Ralphie, Junior's friend. Remember, he was in the bed next to Junior when Junior was in the hospital? And 'course he limps. The boy's got an artificial leg."

"I'm too upset to remember anything." She sighed deeply. "I didn't mean that the way it sounded."

"I know, but him and his brothers were the first ones here this morning."

"May I have your attention." This was the policeman from the night before. He had on hiking clothes like the rest of them. "Now, our goal for today is to find out where Mary Cantrell lives. Most of you know her as Mad Mary, and most of you know she's been living in these hills for years, but nobody knows where.

"It seems pretty obvious that yesterday she took the youngest Blossom boy—Junior; and it's likely that she took him to wherever she lives. Now, if you find out where she is, you come to me or Pap Blossom."

On the porch Pap raised his hand so everyone would know who he was.

"Both Mr. Blossom and I know Mad—Miss Cantrell, and would like to be the ones to approach her. The last thing we want to do is scare her. I don't have to tell you that if she got a mind to take off and hide, we never would find her and the boy. She knows these woods a lot better than we do. Any questions?"

There was a pause. Mist was still lying low on the ground, but overhead it had started to burn off. Beyond, patches of bright blue sky were beginning to show through.

Ralphie raised his hand.

The policeman said, "Yes?"

"This isn't exactly a question," Ralphie said, "but my uncle hunts a lot and one time he almost shot Mad Mary on Owl Hill. It was deer season and she was wearing something brown. Anyway, he said he thinks she lives somewhere around there. She scooted off toward the north."

"That's good information. Your uncle couldn't be here today?"

"He works the early shift, but he may come later."

"Fine. We can use him. No more questions? Then let's get going. We'll pair off at the coyote trap."

And in a body they crossed the yard and headed into the dripping trees.

As soon as Ralphie heard that they would be pairing off, he decided two things. One, he would get rid of his little brothers, and two, he would be the one to pair off with Maggie Blossom.

He had had his eye on Maggie ever since his mom had dropped off the three of them early that morning. "Ralphie, you look after your brothers," his mother had said.

"Mom, I'm here to search for Junior, not be a baby-sitter."

"Remember what I said. The only way I'd let you come is if your brothers came too."

"I know."

"Well, you aren't acting like it." She looked at the brothers. "You stick with Ralphie."

"We will," they chimed.

About a half hour after his mom had driven off, Ralphie decided to lay the groundwork for getting rid of his brothers. "See that girl," he said, "the one on the porch?"

They said, "Yes."

Maggie was still standing on the porch steps. She only had one braid this morning, and she had been chewing on the end of it—out of nervousness, Ralphie figured—when he and his brothers had arrived. The moment she had seen him get out of the car, though, she had flung the braid back over her shoulder and looked down at the ground. She had not even waved, and she had not looked up one single time. Now she was staring at her foot, swinging it over the lower step.

"See the girl I'm talking about?"

The brothers nodded.

"Well, don't get close to her."

"Why?"

"I don't want to tell you. You'll get scared and want to go home."

"No we won't."

"Promise?"

They nodded solemnly.

"Well, she hates little boys, and if you get close to her she'll bite your ears off."

"No she won't."

"She's got a whole belt made out of them."

"That's not true."

"Yes it is too. She was a counselor at a boys' camp, and nobody noticed till they were getting on the bus to go home that none of the little boys had any ears left."

"That is not true."

"Yes it is. The policeman over there told me. You saw me talking to him, didn't you? Well, that was what we were talking about. He asked me to keep an eye on her and to make sure she didn't get close to you. So you go with someone else."

"No. Anyway, I don't believe you. I'm going to ask her if she has a belt made out of boys' ears."

"Oh, never mind. Come on back." Color flushed Ralphie's ears. "Come back! Listen, I was just kidding."

But before Ralphie could stop him, the little brother was at the porch. "Do you have a belt made out of little boys' ears?"

Maggie looked down at him. Maggie had noticed Ralphie as soon as he'd arrived. She had been so glad to see him it had made her feel bad. Nobody should feel happy when their brother is lost. She was trying to make herself feel better by explaining to herself that the reason she was so glad to see him was that if anybody could find Junior, he could. She was saying to herself, Remember how he took over last summer and made everything come out all right? when Ralphie's brother asked about the belt. "What?" she said.

"Do you have a belt made out of little boys' ears? My brother said you do, but I don't believe him."

"Out of what?"

"Little boys' ears." He took his ears in his hands and wiggled them.

"Oh, ears." Maggie nodded. "Yes."

"You do?"

"Yes."

"Where is it, then?"

"Hanging up in my closet."

The little brother came running back across the yard.

"She says yes. She says she does. She says it's in her closet."

Maggie looked right at Ralphie, the first time she had looked at him since he'd arrived. Then she grinned. Ralphie's heart almost turned a flip in his chest. She still had her lovely chipped tooth.

Chapter Twenty-two
The Blossom and the Ball
🌿 🌿 🌿

THE FACE WASN'T QUITE AS BAD AS JUNIOR HAD RE-
membered. He had taken his hands off his eyes as soon
as Mad Mary had said, "Is there something wrong with
your eyes. Let me see."

"No," he had cried, dropping his hands instantly.
"They're fine!"

He removed his hands—they were stiff at his sides
now—but he didn't look at her face. He couldn't. He
looked at her boots. He recalled with a slight shudder
the way he had clutched one the night before.

The boots were coming closer. He swallowed aloud.
Closer. Now she was there, directly in front of him, and
she said, "Who locked you up in that cage?"

The question surprised him so much that he looked
directly up at her face. That was when he saw that it
wasn't as bad as he had thought. "I wasn't in any cage."

"What was it, then?"

"A trap."

"Then who locked you in the trap?"

"Nobody."

94

"Nobody?"

"It locked itself."

"What are you telling me?"

"I made the trap. I was going to catch that coyote everybody's been talking about and get the reward, one hundred dollars. I had it all figured out. I made the trap just perfect—you saw it. Every part of it was perfect. Only, while I was setting the trap, the hamburger meat got stuck on my hand, and the trap sprang and the door slammed down and I couldn't get out."

"Oh, dear," Mad Mary said.

"What's wrong?"

"Oh, dear."

"Why do you keep saying that?"

Mad Mary's look sharpened. "Who are you?"

"Junior. Junior Blossom."

"Are you kin to Alec Blossom?"

"That's Pap, my grandfather. Why?"

"Because I hope he comes looking for you instead of the police."

"Why?"

"Because over the years, Junior, the police have not been kind to Mary."

Mud lay curled in a ball of misery.

Since dawn he had been watching the clearing without hope. The only living thing he had seen was blue jays and squirrels.

All Mud's life he had hated squirrels. He hated them so much that a couple of times he had run headlong into trees trying to catch one. This morning he did not care.

95

He would not have felt like chasing a squirrel, even if he could have.

Sometimes, in happier days, he had chased blue jays, too, but only when someone like Pap said, "Mud! What's that bird doing stealing our worms?" He had never actually caught anything.

The gnats had found Mud and hovered over him, drawn by the wet heat. His fur steamed in the early-morning sunshine. Mud usually snapped at gnats and flies and occasionally caught them. Now he didn't care about gnats either.

Mud whined in and out, with every breath. The sound was as constant as the drone of a bee. Mud didn't even know he was whining.

The mist was off the clearing now, and the sun slanted down through the trees.

Mud heard a new noise. He had heard a hundred noises since dawn—a limb falling from a tree, a twig snapping, birds flying, squirrels leaping from tree to tree; so Mud didn't leap up at just one more sound.

Still, there was something different about this sound. He didn't raise his head from his paws, but he lifted one ear, raised one eye.

The noise came again.

Mud lifted his head. Both ears went up, both eyes. Mud got to his feet.

There was another noise. Voices.

Mud's tail had been curled between his legs in despair, and now it straightened. It wagged once.

It was not just voices. It was Pap's voice.

Mud shook himself, threw back his head, and began to bark.

Chapter Twenty-three
Cave Books

❧ ❧ ❧

"Can I ask you something?" Junior said.

Mad Mary nodded.

Junior and Mad Mary were eating breakfast—leftover varmint stew. At first Junior wasn't sure he was hungry, when he saw and heard what it was, but now he was enjoying the stew as much as Mary was. He swallowed and took a drink of water from a Coke bottle.

"Well, I didn't know that witch—" He swallowed the rest of the word and corrected it carefully: "—that people who live in caves read books."

Mad Mary's face almost cracked into a smile. "What else would we read?"

"I don't know. That's why I was asking."

"Yes, I read books. The ones I like best are the ones where people end up living in caves. My favorite's *Riders of the Purple Sage.*"

"That doesn't sound like a cave book to me."

"Why, that's one of the best cave books ever written. Venters—that's the cowboy—and Bess—that's the rustler girl—live in a cave for months. It's one of the best caves I ever read of. I wish I had one just like it. When the storms used to hit, that cave would gong like a bell. My cave whistles a little, but it never gongs. And rooms— Oh, that cave had more rooms than a mansion."

She wiped her hands on her skirt and smoothed it over her bony knees. "Anyway. That's what I read—books. I don't care for magazines and I don't read newspapers. People who end up living in caves generally don't."

"We don't read newspapers much either, except for the one we were in. Last summer we were news, and I do read that newspaper. I've still got it. Two things happened to us last summer." Junior lifted his hand so he could count them off. "One, we got in the news, and two, we got a telephone."

To this day Junior didn't know which was the most amazing, the fame or the telephone. The installation of the telephone had left Junior with the feeling that he was at last hooked up to the rest of the world, plugged in like everybody else. He loved that telephone.

Sometimes he called strangers on it. "Hello, this is Junior. Have you got time to talk?" he would say. Nobody had so far, but Junior didn't mind. "I'll try you later," he'd say. "So long."

"Over the last ten years," Mad Mary said, looking thoughtful, "I've wanted to call somebody up maybe three times."

"You can use our phone anytime you want to," Junior said generously. "Just come on over."

Mad Mary shook her head. She didn't wear her hat in the cave, and her long gray hair hung down her back. Without her hat, she didn't look so old to Junior. In fact, she was getting younger and younger somehow as the morning progressed.

"My mom wouldn't mind, really."

"Those people I wanted to call up are all dead." Mad Mary looked at her stew. "You know, I wouldn't mind them being dead so much if I could just call them up on the telephone every now and then."

Junior's mouth dropped open. His own stew was forgotten. He drew in a deep shuddering breath. "If I could call my father . . ." he said. "If I could just call my father . . ."

He couldn't finish. The words hadn't been created to express how much he would benefit from talking to his father for three minutes.

"I don't have a living relative left on this earth," Mad Mary went on. She started eating again. "And Cantrells don't die of old age. My brother died in the war. My mother got thrown by a horse. My father set himself on fire with his pipe and burned himself and the whole house down." She smoothed her skirt again, but slowly this time.

"I may have a cousin living somewhere, but my cousins were accident-prone too. My cousin La Rue scalped herself on an electric fan. Anyway, they're dead to me."

"If I could just talk to my father . . ."

Junior trailed off again. The thought somehow was too big for his brain.

"The last time I wanted to call my daddy was when

99

they widened the road and put the Seven-eleven right where our front porch used to be. My daddy was the only person I could think of that would be as mad as I was. I wanted to hear that old man roar one more time."

Junior appeared to hear Mad Mary for the first time.

"I wouldn't want to hear my father roar. I'd just want to hear him say 'Junior, Junior, Junior. What are we going to do with you?' He used to say that a lot."

Mad Mary looked down at him. She closed her weak eye to bring his features in focus. Then she reached over and tapped his hand. "Your stew's getting cold."

"Oh, yes."

"You won't have stew like that very often."

"I know."

"So take advantage of it. Eat. Eat!"

"I will in a minute." He squinted at her as if he wanted to see better too. "What did your dad die of?"

"I told you. He burned himself up and the house too."

"Mine got gored by a bull."

She nodded slightly, but Junior felt the understanding behind that nod. "Now eat."

Junior ate.

Chapter Twenty-four
The Search for Junior

"WILL YOU PLEASE GIVE ME A BREAK AND DO YOUR searching somewhere else?"

"No way. Mom told us to stay together and not get lost."

"And that's what we're going to do too. And, anyway, Maggie told us she does not bite little boys' ears off. So there!"

All morning Ralphie had been trying to get rid of his little brothers and be alone with Maggie. Ralphie was in love with Maggie.

He had fallen in love with her exactly one year ago when he had awakened in the hospital one morning. There she had been, sitting on the foot of her brother's bed, grinning, telling about how she and her other brother had busted into city jail.

Even today, a whole year later, the memory of how wonderful she had been and how stupid he had been could turn the tips of his ears red with embarrassment. "Excuse me for being nosy"—this was one of the stupid things he had said—"but why didn't you just go in the jail and ask to see your grandfather like anybody else?"

"We Blossoms," she had answered, "have never been just anybody."

Well, that was the truth.

"All right," Ralphie said to his brothers, "I'll pay you to leave me alone." He was desperate.

The search for Junior was the first legitimate excuse to see Maggie he had had all year. All the rest of his excuses—like pretending to be in the neighborhood on an errand when, actually, he had ridden six miles on an old bike to get there—had not worked. Maggie had blinked those green eyes and said, "What was the errand?" "Just something for my mom." "What?" "Oh, nothing." His ears turned red a lot around Maggie.

"How much?" the bigger brother said.

"One dollar."

Ralphie intended that later, when he actually had to fork over, he would pretend he had meant a dollar between them. The little brother read his thoughts. "One dollar each?"

Ralphie was truly desperate. Maggie had gone on without him. If he didn't leave right this minute, he might lose her in the woods. "Each."

They extended their hands, palms up.

"Not now. When we get home. Now go on. Go on."

"Ralphie?" It was Maggie calling him. "Are you coming?"

Hobbling up the hill on his artificial leg wasn't easy, but Ralphie hobbled. "Coming!" he called with sudden cheer.

For the first time in his life Ralphie would be alone with the woman he loved.

Mad Mary and Junior were on the rocky ledge in front of the cave—the porch, Mad Mary called it. Mad Mary was in her rocking chair. This was the only piece of family furniture she had. It was a porch rocker, and that was why it hadn't been burned up in the fire.

Junior was lying on his back. They were both watching the vultures overhead.

The vultures must have been two miles up in the sky, Junior figured. He had never seen anything like it. He had never known birds had fun like that, wheeling round and round, never flapping their wings a single time, getting higher with each turn.

"Oh, wow," Junior said. These words—*Oh, wow*—had been the first words Junior had spoken as a baby, and he had used them all the time back then. "Here's a cracker, Junior." "Oh, wow." "Here's a ham sandwich?" "Oh, wow."

The family used to tease him about it, so now he only used the words when he was too impressed not to.

Mad Mary broke the spell of the vultures by bracing her hands on the arms of her rocker and starting to get up. "We ought to get going."

Junior glanced at her in surprise. "Why?"

Junior was having one of the most pleasant mornings of his life. Lying on Mad Mary's porch, watching birds enjoy themselves, eating varmint stew. It was like something a person would pay money to do, buy a ticket for. It was the first real vacation of Junior's life.

And after their conversation about calling up their dead fathers on the telephone, Junior had felt very close to Mad Mary.

"To get you back to your folks."

"No hurry," Junior said. "They know I'm all right."

The last thing Junior wanted was to get back to his folks. First of all, they would want to hear what had happened, and he would have to start with the unfortunate incident of his trapping himself. It was far, far nicer to lie in peaceful silence with Mary and watch the birds.

Junior changed the subject. "Do the vultures fly like that every morning."

"Just when the air's right." Mad Mary leaned back. "Vultures have a bad reputation," she said. "Most people don't like them."

"I do," said Junior. "I like them a lot."

"I do too."

Mad Mary was glad to lean back and put off returning Junior. This was the first human company she had enjoyed in ten years.

"Down in the tropics people can't get along without vultures."

"Why?"

"They eat dead things, keep the jungle clean."

"I didn't know that."

"They never kill anything. Never hurt a living soul, just eat what's already dead, the way I do. I enjoy the competition."

"I would too."

"Over in India—I read this in one of my books, I

never saw it for myself—over in India they have towers where they put dead bodies, and the vultures come down and eat the flesh and then the dry bones drop down into the towers—very sanitary."

Junior's mouth dropped open. "I wish I could read that book."

He looked back up at the sky. Now the vultures had begun a long, slow circling descent. Two more vultures joined them. "They must have spotted lunch," Mad Mary said.

"Do you still have that book?"

"Which one, the vultures or the cave."

"Both."

"They're in there somewhere," Mad Mary said, nodding toward her cave. "I'll try to find them for you." Then she added, "In case you come back."

"Oh, I'll come back," Junior said. "I love it here."

Chapter Twenty-five
Dried Mud

❧　❧　❧

"LET ME HELP YOU," RALPHIE SAID. HE HELD OUT ONE hand. Maggie looked from his hand to the log she was getting ready to step over.

"It's just a log," she said.

"I know, but a person could fall stepping over a log."

"Not me."

"Well, would you please let me help you? I'd like to help you. All right?"

Ralphie's whole face was red now. For fifteen minutes he had been working up the courage to offer to help her over something, and then he had to pick a log, a stupid log, and it wasn't even a big stupid log.

Maggie looked up at him. She grinned, showing her chipped front tooth. "Oh, all right."

"You will?"

She reached out and put her hand in Ralphie's. He gasped with pleasure. For a moment he was so overcome that he forgot why he had offered his hand.

"So help me over the log," Maggie reminded him,

107

grinning again. "That's what we're holding hands for, isn't it?"

"Sure."

Actually Ralphie just stood there, grinning, while she stepped over the log herself. It was such a pleasant experience that Ralphie would have liked nothing better than to keep on helping her over things the rest of his life, but she took her hand back.

"That's enough help," she said, then turned and ran up the hill.

"Wait for me," he called after her.

At last Mud was beginning to dry out. He still paused to give himself a shake every now and then, one of his full body shakes that started at his shoulders and ended at the tip of his tail; but the sun and all the running around had left him almost dry.

The first thing Mud had done when he'd realized he was at last out of the trap had been to run. He had run for half an hour. He didn't run anyplace in particular. He just ran fast, around and around, making huge circles through the trees and back into the clearing, back into the trees, back into the clearing. He barked as he ran.

"Mud's crazy," Vicki said when Mud tore into the clearing for the tenth time.

"You'll have to start calling him Mad instead of Mud," Ralphie said to Maggie.

Maggie smiled, and Ralphie thought it was like having the sun come out. He wanted to say something else funny more than he had ever wanted anything in his life. As usual, when he was around Maggie, his mind didn't work.

"Let the dog run," Pap said. "I'd be running around like that, too, if I'd been locked up in a coyote trap all night."

By the time the crowd was organized and ready to leave the coyote trap, Mud was through running. The crowd began pairing up. Mud didn't hesitate. He knew who he was going to pair up with. Mud got with Pap.

"You know what we're doing this for, Mud, don't you?" Pap asked him as they started through the trees.

Mud wagged his tail.

"We're doing this to find Junior. This ain't just the usual walking in the woods. This is to find Junior. And we'll not enjoy ourselves until we do."

Wagging his tail in agreement, Mud took the lead.

Chapter Twenty-six

Ralphie's Luck

JUNIOR AND MAD MARY WERE ON THE PORCH. THEY were getting ready to leave again. This was the fourth time they had gotten ready, and they were really going this time.

"I wish we didn't have to go yet," Junior said, looking around at the ledge, the cave, the vultures—all the things he had come to treasure.

"Well, we do. We've put it off long enough. They're probably searching for you, and it'll be better for both of us—especially me—if when they find us, it looks like I'm bringing you back."

"You are bringing me back."

"Well, it wouldn't be the first time a person got arrested because of the way something looked. And folks are generally suspicious of me. In town they call me Mad Mary." Junior tried to look as if he never had. "I tell you one thing. I couldn't stand to be put in a cell. That's the reason I got you out and brought you here. Being put in a cage would be the worst thing that would happen to me."

"They couldn't arrest you and put you in jail. You helped me. You can't get arrested for helping somebody."

"You know I was helping you, and I know that, but they don't. They are who counts right now. Come on." Mad Mary pulled her shoulder bag tighter on her shoulder.

They started down the slope, through the fissure in the limestone—like steps, Junior thought. Halfway down, Junior paused and looked up the cliff to the cave, the porch, the curtain of laurel.

Beyond, on a high dead tree one of the vultures sat, sunning himself. It was the most beautiful sight Junior could remember seeing. Last summer Junior had finally gotten out of the habit of saying good-bye to buildings and places. But now he couldn't help it. "Good-bye, cave. I'll be back."

"You coming or not?" Mary said.

Junior nodded. "Anyway," he said as he followed, "if they should arrest you, my brother knows how to bust into jail."

"I hope"—and this time a smile did crack Mad Mary's face—"it won't quite come to that."

"Me too," said Junior.

Ralphie was having very bad luck. He had just figured that enough time had passed since he had helped Maggie over the log, so that he could offer his assistance again. He didn't want to overdo assisting, though. "May I help you over this log? This fern? This twig? This pebble?" That's exactly what Ralphie wanted to do, so he forced himself to wait perhaps longer than necessary.

He was surprised and delighted that at that moment he and Maggie came to a small stream. Perfect. He was just getting ready to step across and offer his hand. Maybe he wouldn't even have to say the words. Maybe Maggie would just accept the wordless offer. At that magic moment, when the whole world seemed to be cooperating in his romance, Vern came crashing down the hill.

Ralphie was so startled that he stumbled and fell sideways into the creek. Pain shot through the stump of his leg. He was glad the water was icy because at least that kept him from fainting.

Vern said excitedly, "Pap says he thinks it's Vulture Roost."

"What?"

"Where Mad Mary lives. He remembered there's a cave there. He says his daddy took him there one time and told him it was an old Indian cave. Come on!"

Ralphie would have been glad to come on, but he didn't think he could get up. Vern was already scrambling back up the hill now, so it was obvious he wouldn't help.

Ever since Ralphie had cut off his leg with the riding mower, he had not let his artificial leg stop him from doing one single thing. He even played Little League and slid into bases with the best of them. For the first time, there in the creek at Maggie's feet, he would have given anything to have his own leg back.

At that moment, the absolute lowest of his life, he

looked up and saw a beautiful sight. It was Maggie and she was offering her hand to him. She was offering her hand! Ralphie took it and she pulled him up.

And the best part, Ralphie thought, as they started up the hill, still holding hands, the best part was that this time she didn't have a good excuse for taking her hand back. She couldn't say "That's enough help" because this time she had offered.

"How's your leg?" Maggie asked.

Wisely he answered, "It still hurts."

"Let me know when it stops."

"I will," he said.

Chapter Twenty-seven
Baby Vultures

🌿* 🌿* 🌿*

JUNIOR AND MAD MARY WERE COMING AROUND THE old quarry. They skirted the crumbling sandstone.

"I know it's wrong to wish this," Junior said.

"What?"

"Well, I wish I could have a baby vulture."

"There's nothing wrong with wishing for that."

"There isn't?"

"No, I had one one time. It fell out of its nest and it lived with me for two months. I taught it how to fly. For all I know it might have been one of those vultures we watched this morning."

"I bet it was nice to have a baby vulture."

"Yes and no," said Mad Mary. She was using her long stick so easily that Junior wanted a long stick too. He paused to find one. When he fell in behind her again, she was saying, "When I found that baby vulture, the first thing I did was try and put it back in the nest. The parents wouldn't let me get close. They make a hissing sound, then a rattle, like a rattlesnake. I gave up after a while and took the baby home. The bad part about a baby vulture is that when it gets scared or upset, it vomits up everything it's eaten. If you could train them not to do that, well, they would make as nice a pet as a parrot."

"You know something?" Junior said.

"Yes, I know a thing or two." Mad Mary's lined face cracked into another smile. "What exactly did you have in mind?"

Junior paused to get his thoughts straight. He wanted to say this right.

"Well, you probably don't know this, but at my school a lot of kids have spend-the-nights. Like, one kid will invite another kid over to spend the night."

"They had those when I was growing up, too, but I never went to one. My daddy wouldn't let me."

Junior frowned. He was not getting his message across. What he wanted was for Mad Mary to get the idea to invite him for a spend-the-night.

"Actually," he went on, "probably anybody could have a spend-the-night. It wouldn't have to be a kid. It could be a—well, anybody. For example—"

Ahead Mad Mary stopped and held up one hand. Junior had been so intent on the wording of his spend-the-night request that he'd walked directly into her back.

"What is it?"

"Here they come."

"What? Who?" Junior sputtered.

"People," Mad Mary said.

Mud was in the lead. He had been all morning. He was not sure what they were looking for, but he knew he would know it when he saw it.

He came loping through the trees and into a small clearing. He stopped cold. There, right in front of him, piercing him with her wild eyes, was Mad Mary.

Her cane was raised in the air as if to strike him. Her face, her stance, her eyes, all threatened.

Mud's lips pulled back in a snarl. There were only three people in Alderson County that Mud had no use for. Two of them were the Brownlee brothers who used him occasionally for target practice with their BB guns. The other was Mad Mary.

He didn't know why he didn't like her. She had never actually done anything to him. He just didn't like her, that was all, and every time he and Pap saw her on their can-collecting rounds, the fur would rise on his back. Pap would say, "That is a friend of mine, Mud. Hush! Behave yourself or get back in the truck."

This time Pap wasn't there to make him behave. Pap was a hundred yards back, staggering through the trees with a hand over his heart.

Mud growled and got ready to spring.

Chapter Twenty-eight

Gone

❧   ❧   ❧

THE NEXT FEW SECONDS WERE TO JUNIOR LIKE THE trap springing shut all over again. One moment it had been he and Mary walking along happily, enjoying themselves, chatting about baby vultures, and then Mud had appeared.

He had come charging through the trees in a long noiseless lope, so they hadn't even heard him. And now he was right in front of them in a sort of crouch that Junior had never seen before.

And that wasn't all that was wrong. In fact, nothing about Mud looked right. For one thing, he was snarling. Junior had never seen so much of Mud's teeth. He could even see the gums. And the low growls raised the hair on Junior's neck. He was glad to be behind Mad Mary.

Mad Mary was still as death. She said, "Is that your dog?" in a flat voice. She was different somehow too.

He didn't want to claim Mud, but he said, "I think so."

"Then you're all right."

117

And in a swirl of skirts—it was as if she really were a witch—Mad Mary ducked into a wall of laurels and disappeared.

"Wait!"

Junior tried to follow her into the laurels, but Mud was jumping on him now, licking his face, panting, barking. His hot breath infuriated Junior.

"Stop breathing on me. Go on, get away," Junior cried, struggling with the leaves.

How had Mary slipped in so easily? He couldn't get past the first limb. It was like something in a story, not one of Mad Mary's wonderful stories where people ended up living in caves but one of those awful magic stories where somebody slipped into another century and you couldn't follow no matter how hard you tried.

"Go on!" he said to Mud as if Mud were holding him back, not the thick laurels.

Then Pap grabbed him. Pap's old fumbling hands turned him around.

"Pap!" He yelled it not because he was glad to see him but because he wanted Pap to let him go.

Pap pulled Junior against him. Over Junior's head he yelled, "I found him. He's all right. Junior's all right. Here he is, everybody!"

Pap was patting him on the back, hard, as if he were trying to knock something out of Junior's windpipe. "Oh, is your mother going to be happy. Vicki, he's fine! Somebody tell Vicki he's fine!"

Then he bent his radiant face to look more closely at Junior. "What happened? Did you get lost? I figured Mary had you."

"She did."

Junior glanced, now without hope, at the laurels. Movement far up the slope caught his eye, and he looked up, shielding his eyes. If the movement had been her, she was gone.

"I figured she'd take good care of you. Everybody else was worried, but I went to school with Mary. She was real gentle."

"She still is." This time Junior's voice wavered.

"Now, don't you cry." Pap patted his shoulder. "You're safe now. You're going home."

That was what Junior was afraid of. And when his mom came bursting through the trees, he could barely make her out through his tears.

Chapter Twenty-nine
Back at the Cave

✦ ✦ ✦

"JUNIOR, ARE YOU STILL MOPING ABOUT THAT COYOTE getting caught?" Pap asked.

Junior said, "No."

"Fool coyote trapped himself, squeezed into a henhouse, swallowed a couple of hens, and couldn't squeeze out. And, Junior, the coyote never even got close to where your trap was at. You never even stood a chance of trapping anything but yourself and Mud."

"I know that. I wish everybody would quit talking about it."

"Well, they would if you'd quit moping."

"I'm not moping!"

There was a pause while Pap watched Junior. "Are you moping over Mary?" he asked finally.

"Maybe." Junior's shoulders sagged. "I didn't even get to say good-bye or anything, and I can't find my way back. And she was going to lend me a book."

"I'll take you to see Mary if you'll stop moping and eat your breakfast," Pap said.

121

Junior looked up. He brushed tears from his eyes. "Will you really?"

Pap nodded.

"I don't see what's so great about seeing Mad Mary again," Vern said. Vern was sitting across from them at the table. He had not eaten any of his breakfast either, but no one had noticed. Not one single person was trying to make him stop moping.

"You couldn't," Junior explained, "because you weren't there."

"No, but I've seen her. I see her all the time on the road. The kids at school say she's a witch."

"Well, she is not."

"Let him go if he wants to," Maggie said.

"And anyway," Junior said. He was eating now, fast. He swallowed. "Anyway, she promised to lend me two of her books."

"Lend you books? You're walking all the way out there to borrow books? Big deal!"

"These are very special books. You wouldn't understand."

"Did I hear right?" Vicki Blossom said, entering the kitchen. "You're going to take him back out to that old woman's cave?"

"She ain't old. She's my age."

"Pap, you don't need to walk all that way. Your leg's still bothering you. If it's a book he wants, Maggie can take him to the public library."

"They wouldn't have these books," Junior said. "One's about vultures and one's about caves. And even if they did have them," he went on, "they wouldn't be the same."

Pap sat down on a boulder and put one hand over his heart. "Me and Vern will wait here. You go the rest of the way by yourself."

"Don't you want to see her?"

"I can live without it," Pap said. "I imagine she can live without seeing me too."

"I think she'd want to see you."

"Me and Vern'll wait."

"Well, all right, if you really don't want to."

Junior turned toward the cave. Overhead, vultures wheeled in the sky, making—it seemed to Junior—welcoming circles.

"Those are the vultures I was telling you about." He turned his bright face to Pap and Vern. "When they spot something to eat, they'll start down. You can watch them while I'm gone."

Junior took a few steps toward the cave. He turned again. The sun was in his eyes, so he shaded them. "Pap?"

"What?"

"What do I do if she's not there. Wait?"

"Yeah. When we have to start back, I'll whistle for you."

Junior walked around the outcropping of limestone and picked his way carefully over the loose stones. He kept looking up, trying to spot the cave.

It was odd. The cave seemed to have disappeared. In his mind it had been the most obvious thing in the world. The porch stuck out like a real porch. The door behind was square like a real door.

He stumbled on a stone. Is that it? Again he shaded his eyes.

High up on the cliff, just beneath the spines of limestone, was a ledge. Was it the ledge? He walked more slowly, dragging his feet. Suddenly he saw a rocking chair on the ledge, and in the rocking chair . . .

Junior broke into a run. "I'm back!" he called happily.

"You sure took your time," she answered, getting up from her rocking chair to meet him.

Chapter Thirty
Hello, Mad Mary

VERN SAT ON THE BOULDER BESIDE PAP. HIS SHOUL-
der touched Pap's arm, but Vern had never felt more
alone in his life.

For one thing, it had never occurred to Vern that he
and Pap wouldn't go up to the cave, wouldn't get to see
all the wonders Junior had been bragging about all
week. It was bad enough not to see where Mad Mary
cooked and slept and ate, not to see the boxes of books,
the famous rocking chair.

But what was worse was that, as he sat there on the
sun-warmed boulder, he realized the cold hard truth:
that he alone in the family had no friends. Not one.

He went over the other family members, one by one.
Pap had Mud. Maggie had Ralphie and girls at school.
The girls and Ralphie even called Maggie up on the
phone.

Vern went on glumly: Junior had Ralphie, and now he
had Mad Mary. His mom had a lot of new beautician
friends. He had nobody.

"Why do people like Maggie and Junior better than they do me?" he asked finally.

Pap looked at him. "I didn't know they did."

"Well, they do."

"I doubt it. Anyway," Pap said, taking his hand from his heart, "we Blossoms don't need as many friends as most people. We got ourselves."

Vern didn't answer. He could see that Pap wouldn't understand in a million years.

Vern's head snapped up. He had just heard Junior's voice ring out the good news—"I'm back!"—heard the welcome in Mad Mary's voice as she shouted back, "You sure took your time."

He scuffed his foot against the earth. Disgustedly he said, "She's there."

Junior was on the porch with his back to the view, so that he could see Mary. Mary had been in the middle of reading a book when he'd arrived, an old worn book that looked like it had been read a lot. But as soon as she had seen him, she had put the book down. Now it lay in her lap. One gnarled finger marked her place.

"Been making any more traps?"

"No."

"That's good."

"They caught the coyote in a henhouse. I might make something else, though. I like to make things." He squinted up at her. "Is there anything you need? I'll make you something."

"I got everything I want."

"Me, too, except a bike. Bikes are hard to make."

"I imagine."

"I made a unicycle one time, but I hurt myself real bad when I tried to ride it."

Mad Mary almost smiled again.

"Did you make things when you were little?"

"No, I used to spend my time playing house. I'd spend hours setting up little rooms out in the yard, under the trees. I'd mark off the walls in the dirt, and set tables with acorns and leaves. I guess I'm still doing the same thing—playing house."

Junior nodded.

A bobwhite whistled and Junior lifted his head. "I think that was Pap."

"Your granddad came with you?"

"Yes, he was afraid I couldn't find my way without help. I couldn't then, but I could now. He's waiting at the bottom of the cliff, he and my brother."

"Well, why didn't they come up?"

"Pap said you might not want to see them."

"I wouldn't mind." She braced her arms on her rocking chair and started to get up. Then she sat back down. "You know something?"

Junior grinned. "I know some things. What did you have in mind?"

She grinned too. Her teeth were older looking than her face, but still Junior thought she was prettier when she smiled.

"Getting you out of that cage and bringing you back here was the best thing I ever did."

Junior was flattered. He didn't get that many compliments. A flush of pleasure ran through his body.

"I was about in a cage myself, and getting you out of yours was the start of me getting out of mine."

Junior didn't understand, but he nodded with what he considered his wise look—eyes half closed, mouth serious.

"Wait a minute. I got your books." She got them from the cave and gave them to Junior. "I'll walk down with you and say hello to your folks."

Junior scrambled to his feet. Mad Mary's two books were clutched against his heart. "They would be honored," he said.

It was Vern who had made Pap give the whistle. He'd kept saying "He's been there long enough," and "Let's go," and "Well, how long do we have to wait?" and "What are we waiting for, Christmas?" until finally he had worn Pap down, and Pap had given a whistle for Junior.

Now Vern was standing with his hands jammed in his pockets, staring glumly at his feet. He was thinking that the worst part of the afternoon was yet to come—listening to Junior's ravings on the long walk home. Mad Mary this— No, Mary this and Mary that. Vern didn't think he could stand it. At that moment, the absolute low point of the afternoon, he heard Pap say, "Well, Mary, it's good to see you. It's been a while."

He looked up. There she was, so close he could have reached out and touched her. He could even smell her. She had a sort of wild animal odor. It wasn't, he thought, anything that could be corrected with deodorant; it was a way-of-life sort of smell.

"Mary, this is my other grandson, Vern."

"Pleased to meet you," he muttered. He wiped his hand on his pants in case she was expecting to shake, but she wasn't. He breathed with relief.

"How's can collecting, Alec?" she asked.

"Well, this here's the season for it. I hope you aren't planning to take it up."

"Food collecting takes about all my time."

Junior said, "Vern, did you see the vultures?"

"Yes, you showed them to me before."

"Well, they're still there." He pointed them out again. Junior's eyes were shining. He wanted to take Mary's hand, but he was not sure she would let him. In Junior's mind she was like the grandmother he had never known. Pap's wife, Maida, had died before Junior was even born, and sometimes in stores he ached with longing when he saw grandmothers spoiling their grandchildren. It was strange. Mad Mary was as old as a grandmother, and yet in some ways she was the exact same age he was.

"Well, you all come back when you can stay awhile," Mary said. She turned abruptly and started up the limestone steps.

"We will," Junior called after her.

Vern kept watching. The pain of not having a friend had somehow become the determination to get one, maybe one better than Ralphie or Mad Mary, if that was possible. In his mind the year ahead was labeled like the Chinese years they had talked about last year in school. The Year of the Bear. The Year of the Lotus. The Year of the Friend.

"Well, let's start walking," Pap said. "Mud's going to be wondering what happened to us. That dog's got more sense than most people. He knew I was going to shut him up in the cellar even before I did. I couldn't even trick him to get him down there. I had to push him down and shut the door on him. I hated to see his face when I done it."

"Well, he couldn't come, Pap. He snarled at Mary last time and chased her off."

"I know, but I sure hated to see the look on his face."

Chapter Thirty-one
Good-bye, Blossoms

"HOLD YOUR HEAD STILL," VICKI TOLD MAGGIE, "AND quit trying to look out the window."

"Well, hurry," Maggie said.

"You can't hurry French braids."

"You're the one who wanted me to have French braids. I would have been happy with ponytails."

"You'll like them when I get through. Next week I'm going to do cornrows."

"Mom, Pap and Vern are going to leave me. I think I hear them getting in the truck."

"I thought you didn't like to go can collecting."

"Well, I do. Everybody knows us now. Everybody rolls down their car window and yells 'Hello, Blossoms' when they see us. I like it."

"Is Junior going?"

Vicki tugged Maggie's head around—Maggie was trying to look out the window again. "They are getting in the truck, Mom. Hurry."

"They'll wait. I asked is Junior going."

"No."

"Why not?"

"He said he was busy."

Vicki started braiding Maggie's hair more slowly. "Busy doing what?"

"I don't know. He won't let us see."

Vicki stopped braiding altogether. "Where is Junior?"

"In the barn."

"Not again. I'll be right back."

"Mom, don't leave me. My hair's only half done! Mom!"

Vicki Blossom ran out onto the porch and down the steps. She ran across the yard. Junior had tugged the barn door closed for privacy, and his mom yanked it open.

"Whatever you're doing or making, Junior, stop it right this minute."

"Bye, Mom," Maggie called quickly.

Vicki glanced around, and she threw up her hands when she saw Maggie getting in the truck. "Maggie, you can't go off with your hair half braided. Now people recognize you as a Blossom. You got to look right!"

"I'll finish it myself on the way," Maggie called. Then she said "Scoot over" to Vern.

"No way. I'm sitting by the window."

"Oh, all right, if you want to be selfish." She crawled over his legs.

Pap gave Mud's honk—one long, two shorts—and Mud came running out of the barn. Without breaking

stride, he leapt into the back of the truck and faced forward.

Pap started the truck and made a broad U-turn in the dusty yard. "Oh, go on," Vicki Blossom said, waving them away. She entered the barn.

"Junior," she said, "you and I are going to have to have a little talk. Now I am not going through another one of these Blossom Julys. I am too old." She couldn't see for a moment, the sun had been too bright outside. Then her eyes adjusted to the dim barn. She put her hands on her hips.

"All right, Junior," she said. "What in the world is that?"

About the Author

With over twenty books to her credit, Betsy Byars has been lauded throughout her career. In 1970 her *Summer of the Swans* won the Newbery Medal, and in 1980 her first book for Delacorte Press, *The Night Swimmers,* won the American Book Award for juvenile fiction. Delacorte Press has also published *The Animal, The Vegetable, and John D Jones,* and *The Not-Just-Anybody Family,* which is a companion volume to *The Blossoms Meet the Vulture Lady.* Ms. Byars is a licensed pilot and lives in Clemson, South Carolina.